Narcissus

J. Earl Loving Jr

Order this book online at www.trafford.com
or email orders@trafford.com

Most Trafford titles are also available at major online book retailers.

Note for Librarians: A cataloguing record for this book is available from Library
and Archives Canada at www.collectionscanada.ca/amicus/index-e.html

Printed in Victoria, BC, Canada.

ISBN: 978-1-4251-5216-1 (soft)
ISBN: 978-1-4251-5217-8 (ebook)

*Our mission is to efficiently provide the world's finest, most comprehensive book publishing
service, enabling every author to experience success. To find out how to publish your book, your
way, and have it available worldwide, visit us online at www.trafford.com*

Trafford rev. 8/10/2009

 www.trafford.com

North America & international
toll-free: 1 888 232 4444 (USA & Canada)
phone: 250 383 6864 ♦ fax: 812 355 4082

Narcissus:

PREFACE
By Harold P. Jones

Well, here I am Harold P. Jones talking about Earl's new book. But before I get to that, let me tell you. I just about bragged to all my boyfriends about that first book of his, because it is a good one and I helped a little. But do you know that some of them boys would not even read it. A couple of them never learned how to read, so if they can't, they can't! But then you got them Negroes that know everything. but even them intelligent ones I mean the ones that got their noses in the newspapers and talking how they would change their people, other people's families, churches, and the world. So, I am a little disappointed with my boyfriends as I feel that clues to doing all these things may be in Earl's book The Whispers of The Streets, if not answers perhaps some of the questions we should be asking.

My granddaughter still keeps telling me to call my boyfriends something else like buddies. She says that calling them boyfriends may cause some people to think I am gay. I always laugh when she says something stupid like that, because a man does not have to worry about what people think which is another thing Earl and I discussed.

Anyway, even though, I tried. Many of them don't read nothing! So what you going to do? My granddaughter who was in the beginning was proud of the book, now sees it and Earl differently. It looks like some of her friends done told her that it ain't perfect.

I told her that the thing I am proud of is that he did it and it is a great story. So she just looked at me and walked away. I never brought it up to her again, because like I said, she comes over and feeds me and kicks the dust around a little.

Earl and I still talk. He tells me about signing the book in lots of places like book stores, hotels, book clubs, colleges, universities, bars and clubs; anywhere there are interested people. He has been in several states talking about, selling and signing books. He is very proud of the facts that there are readers in most of these United States and even in some foreign countries. I asked him how many he sold, and he just laughed.

He told me that writing and publishing his book (with my help) had to be divinely inspired as he never in his wildest dream thought he would pull it off. He is convinced that God sent angels to help, and encourage him to write it. Some of these angels were human and have gone on to help others. After the book was written, he said that the only person who believed it would be published was he. After he published it, there were plenty of people who pointed out to him the reasons it would not succeed. They said that nobody was going to pay for it, and it was not flawless. He laughed and said that the vast majority of folk I know of finished the novel. Even people who do not like me too much, enjoyed the book. And as he was leaving he said, the thousands of folk who have read and talked about my book outweigh those others.

This new book of his, called Narcissus, is a continuation of his book. He says that he had more fun with it, and many of the characters really cut the fool. I have read most of it and have trouble deciding which one I like the most. He will not let me read the end of the book, but I think I know what is going to happen. That's funny because I thought I knew what was going to happen at the end of the other one and was dead wrong.

I hope you enjoy this book and if you have not read the first one, I really think you owe it to yourself. He will probably see that this part is cut out, but I really think we should support the man a lot more. Read the book and learn a little something. Now, here is a poem to kind of warm you up.

THERE AIN'T NO STARS IN CHERRY HILL

By me and my crazy self -KASHEEMA JONES(6TH grader)

There ain't no stars in Cherry Hill which was what I was trying to tell my science teacher who don't live out here with her white self 'cause only us black people live out here 'cause don't nobody else want to be around us or at least that's what my mother tells me while she brushes my hair sometimes when she feels like being my mama, but that's another story.

Anyway, she stood right up there in front of us, saying that the stars are right up there acting like they are a bunch of animals and gods and we could see them if we stood out front of our houses on the lawns and looked up at them at night she told us that was our homework.

Well, I came home and told my mother about going out there at night watching them stars acting like fools which I do not believe anyway.

So, my mama looked at me like she thinks that I do not have nothing else to do but to lie about my fool teacher and her home work.

After she thought about it she sat me down and told me that she could not let me stay up and go outside at night and look up at no stars 'cause there would not be nobody to watch my back in case somebody that can't shoot straight be trying to shoot somebody else and kill me by mistake and she says that she ain't got no money to be burying me and stuff then she pinched me to let me know that she was just kidding.

But she told me that if I wanted I could look out my window to see them animals and things that Miss Andrews be talking about but like I said there ain't no stars in Cherry Hill so when I looked out my window at the late night rain and I see these guys out there fussing about them drugs.

CHERRY HILL IS AN AREA OF BALTIMORE WITH MORE THAN ITS SHARE OF SUBSIDIZED HOUSING AND MANY OF THE CHALLENGES ASSOCIATED WITH FOLK WHO FEEL LEFT OUT.

FORWARD:
NARCISSUS

Although this work is totally fiction, it is believed that work reflects what is and continues to need a lot of attention in our urban communities. This work reflects the good, bad, and ugly in all of us.

Please be reminded that each of us has our share of blame, however we also have the keys to victory over this madness. We can change what often seems to be irreversible.

We can with our faith in the God make our areas filled with hopelessness and despair, places of beauty, spender, and reflect what is great in all of us.

"When a person places the proper value on freedom, there is nothing under the sun that he will not do to acquire that freedom. Whenever you hear a man saying he wants freedom, but in the next breath he is going tell you what he won't do to get it, or what he doesn't believe in doing in order to get it, he doesn't believe in freedom. A man who believes in freedom will do anything under the sun to acquire...or preserve his freedom."

-Malcolm X

"...We are all caught in an inescapable network of mutuality, tied into a single garment of destiny. Whatever affects one directly, affects all indirectly."

Martin Luther King, Jr.

About the Author

This youngster was born on May 9, 1946 to the proud parents of Ann F. and (the late) James Earl Loving Sr. in Baltimore Maryland. He grew up knowing that his parents and extended family loved and supported him. He spent most of his summers in rural Sylvania, Georgia with his maternal grandparents, Bennie and Rosa Foy, along with his numerous family members.

At home and in Georgia, he attended Sunday School and church, regularly, which was required. He learned from the above a strong sense of family and a deep level of religious and spiritual belief (although it was not always apparent).

James Earl Loving Jr. was educated in the Baltimore City School System, graduating from Baltimore City College (high school) in 1964. From 1965 to 1972, he attended, and graduated from Coppin State College (now University) while working too many jobs to mention. He began his teaching career in 1972, most of it in Special Education, at various schools and on various levels. As many do, he found ways to supplement his teaching career by doing other things like bar tending, cab driving, being a bouncer, clerk, auto sales, collections, and other things as he was "earning his PhD's. in the streets."

He has benefited from having great friends, acquaintances, co-workers, and students, but always credits and thanks God for being with him. He knows that God has been with him when in places he should not have been and doing things he should not have done.

Always remember: "Blessings are Irreversible"

Dedications:

This work is dedicated first to Our Lord and Savior Jesus Chris,

To my mother, Annie F. Loving and late father, James E. Loving, Sr. who were always there for us.

To my sister, Annette and brother, Eric

To my countless friends, relatives, and acquaintances on both sides of the River Jordan who loved and helped me over "life's speed bumps."

To those of you who have read, experienced, and enjoyed
"THE WHISPERS of THE STREETS"

To the youngsters who are often misunderstood and misguided because we cannot hear their cries of confusion, despair, and /or their voices of agony.

And finally to those who listen carefully enough to hear the whispers of the streets and desire to help.

Contents

Chapter 1
Mrs. Nadine L. Walker

Just like yours, her best sleep is always right before the sun comes up, those precious moments before the world becomes alive. The dark and quiet exploded into melodic chaos as Mrs. Nadine L. Walker's clock radio rudely woke her at exactly 4:45 a.m. To made matters worse, the disc jockey played and talked over the love song, "Oh What a Night." As painful as it was that she spent all of her nights alone, it was absolute agony that there were no, absolutely no prospects of a man. And oh! Seemed like she would never have the man of her dreams sleeping, holding, and caressing her instead of those damned pillows. The man's sexy voice-overs caused her so much misery that she damned near threw the radio out the window!

As she laughed, he raised his baritone voice to a fever pitch, "Yes, sometimes you want to just stand up in front of the world and testify . . ." The next ballad began, "I stand accused of loving you, too much . . ."

She, who had not been touched by a man for years, moaned, "sure, like hell you love me." As the ballad continued, she thought of those wonderful, naive days when she believed that she and her "ex" would last forever.

She hugged her pillow, slide out of her bed, and danced toward her windows as the singer with his deep baritone voice continued, " . . . I hope I never have to testify, 'cause if I do . . ." She mimicked blowing smoke in a man's ear as she gazed at her reflection in the window. It confirmed that she was drop-dead gorgeous with a body to die for. Her lovely oval face stunned men, so they would not approach her and that was really not her fault.

Nadine turned and danced the naughty dance slowly with her imaginary partner to the bathroom, wondering why she had bothered to put on her robe. The rhythm of his hips and nibbling of her ear was causing beads of perspiration all over her body. She picked up her dropped cigarette, wondering how long her fantasy had lasted and how long her clothes had been off.

When she was finally ready for her shower, she began to think about the day ahead of her. This was the first day for the students with those high-energy seventh graders getting on her damned nerves. She knew she would not have much time to teach any English. She wondered how bad this group would be although she knew some of the student from the prior year, the ones she had to fail. Oh how she wished she could climb back in bed with her imaginary man and forget going to work. However, she needed the money! Boy! Did she need the money!

She examined herself carefully in the full-length mirror. She really liked what she saw, and knew men did too. She disrobed and stepped into the shower with the poise and grace of a well-paid, high fashioned model. She indulged herself by allowing the warm water and liquid soap to caress her body. However, lathering herself caused her to feel "anxious" as it had been years since a man had even touched her. She laughed as she sang, "Baby . . . if I could turn back the hands of time."

As she began feeling uneasy lathering and touching herself, she rushed through rinsing herself and got out of the shower with a lot less ceremony than when she entered. After drying herself, she looked again at herself in the mirror, confirming again that she "had it." After blow-drying and combing her hair, she walked down to the kitchen. Nadine loaded and started her coffee maker for her four or five cups she needed to get started. Teaching really wore on her nerves, she thought as she flipped on the radio.

"Hey now!" she shouted as she began to dance to the upbeat music of the morning show. But that reminded her of the Labor Day cookout she and her daughters had attended the prior day. She hated going to parties where her friends and relatives always tried to fix her up with some fool. Yesterday's Casanova was too short, too young, too dark, too fat, and even worse too, too broke.

"Said he was some kind of mechanic, even had his own shop, but his hands looked so beat up and dirty," she laughed to herself, "so, I told him I needed some mechanic work on my car. He grinned, looking me up and down saying, "bring it pass my shop and we will talk.' " She knew exactly what he meant and was instantly angry, and she told him so. Before she could finish, he bowed his head and walked away which made her angrier!

"I am certainly not . . . sleeping with a grease monkey just to get my car fixed." There was no one close enough to hear her. She looked around hoping no one saw her talking to herself.

While pouring her third cup of coffee, she looked up at the clock 6:10. She called her girlfriend and coworker, Tracey. It rang four or five times, finally she heard the telephone being picked up and dropped to the floor. She heard giggling, loud laughter, and Tracey asking Johnny to stop, so she could answer the phone. This made Nadine so furious that she slammed the telephone back on its cradle, and fussing ". . . all Tracey thinks about is Johnny and sex! You would think . . . after being married as long as they have, they would . . .! Some people!"

She opened the refrigerator to begin fixing lunches for herself and her twin fourteen-year-old girls, Shala and Natra. She really did not like to send them to school with sandwiches, but there was nothing she could do right now! Nadine was just about dead broke, money and gas tank on "E."

She heard and answered the telephone. Cheerful, buoyant, fast talking Tracey began, "Beautiful morning isn't it! Was it you that just called? Johnny is being so bad this morning, telling me he is the teacher's pet and . . .! Stop Johnny before I get Nadine to slap your fingers. Girl, you don't even know!"

3

Not even trying to hide her disdain for their behavior, "Yes I did call, in fact, I really did not mean to disturb you two rabbits, but all I wanted to know is if you wanted me to come get you."

Not noticing her tone, Tracey thanked her, told Nadine she loved her for thinking about her, and she had to get back to Johnny. Nadine heard Tracey's very heavy breathing, "I . . . I . . . will see you when you get here! And Johnny will stop pass his credit union to get the money we will lend you. And . . . ooooooh Johnnnyyyyyyyyy . . ."

Nadine heard the distinct click of the telephone as she thought, "damned, it was never like that for me." She, then, called the girls who always woke up and greeted each other the same way, every day fighting! Thank God! The house was big enough for them to have separate rooms. They looked identical but very different interests and temperaments. They always were at each other's throats.

Shala was the one that she loved. She was quiet, softly spoken, a serious student, and very much the lady. Then there was Natra, the flirt, and the excitable one who got put out of the private school for "...behaviors unbecoming to a young lady." She was holding on in the public school she was attending and seemed to have overcome many of her behaviors.

Shala had to leave earlier via a private school bus, which left Natra to be dropped off to school by Nadine. However, very often Natra would run into and lock the bathroom door just to get on her sister's nerves. They would fight for each other like rabid dogs, but God help anyone who messed with either one of them. They were good girls, but Nadine wished that Natra would spend more time studying like her sister and less time on the telephone. Also, Nadine wished Natra would calm her hot self down!

With her fifth cup in her hand, she passed the antagonists who were standing in the hallway, inches away from each other screaming their hearts out. Shala accused Natra of intentionally using up all the hot water, and invited her to get out of her face. Natra countered, "You don't need hot water with your cold, cold self! Cold water is fine for your 'ain't never had no boyfriend self.' I'm sick and tired of trying to explain to everybody you ain't no lesbo! So, get out of my face and FACE THE COLD WATER!"

"Whatever I am, I really do not care what your low life, gutter dweller friends think. I certainly do not have to make friends with my body." Too through with Natra, she stormed into the bathroom and slammed the door!

Nadine started to talk to them about being so loud and disagreeable, but she dismissed the thought. She went into her room to finish dressing.

Natra stormed into her room with a look of nullification, "I just left downstairs and saw them welfare lunches in the kitchen! You wasted your time fixing mine 'cause. I ain't having it! Why didn't' you get me one of those lunch pales with Snow White and them little punks on it? Why do you want to treat me like a little child? I am going to call Daddy, tell him that I need lunch money, because there is no way I am going to take this!"

"Can't you please just take a lunch this one day? . . .I'all . . ."

"Nope, I have a reputation."

"Why can't you be more like your sister?"

"Duh! You must forget I used to go to that school where they provide, need I repeat pro-vide all meals! Maybe I ought to leave you two here and go live with Daddy until you get yourself together!"

Checkmate!

Nadine reached in her pocketbook and gave Natra four of her last nine dollars. Nadine looked at her wondering where she got her mean streak.

Natra was proud of the way she could always bluff her mother. She would never say anything to anybody including her father about her mother. She would never do anything to hurt her mother, except, maybe, smack Shala in the mouth. "One thing for sure," she thought, "if my child ever pulled up to me like I just did, I'd total her butt and toss it out the door!" Natra left the room without saying a word.

"You are welcome," Nadine said to the empty space.

Now dressed, Nadine posed in front of her full-length mirror. She checked herself from head to toe and was very pleased. She could hear herself being introduced as the star of the high fashioned beauty pageant, "...approaching you now is Ms. Nadine L. Walker!" Applause!

"She is wearing a form-fitting blue with a gold pin striped suit which exposing just enough cleavage to make you wonder if she is naughty or nice. The knee length shirt exposes her shapely legs, which seem to flow into her very stylish blue pumps. Accentuated by a single gold thin necklace, a diamond ring set in gold, gold watch, and small gold earrings she is truly the star of this show." Applause!

She glanced at her watch, 7:02. She deliberately walked down the stairs craving a complement. However, the girls were to busy getting their last shots in before being separated for the day. Natra was describing Shala's uniform as a prison uniform. Shala countered by saying Natra looked just like a tramp, a tramp in heat!

Before Nadine intervened, the OH too welcomed sound of the school bus ended the conflict. Before Shala rushed out of the door, she ran over to her mother, hugged her, smiling broadly, "Looking good, mom!"

Nadine tried to convince her once sleek expensive automobile to start while Natra began singing. Finally, after a few prayers and threats, the car decided to start and off they went tugging along to go pick up Tracey. Nadine wondered again why she even messed with that childish acting woman who was sometimes just a major embarrassment to her.

Tracey was petite, dark complexioned, and as free spirited as Nadine was conservative. Tracey wore jeans, and other clothing that was informal. At twenty-eight, Tracey was about thirteen years younger than Nadine. Tracey usually talked fast with a smile, avoiding drama at all costs, where Nadine saw very little to be happy about. Tracey truly loved and admired Nadine.

As they arrived, Tracey ran down the two flights of steps from her porch, down to the car. As Nadine would have predicted, she was wearing a blue denim blouse and jeans. Natra was so happy to see Tracey that she jumped out of the car to hug and greet Tracey, annoying Nadine.

As the two finally got in the car and before Nadine could voice her displeasure, Tracey began, "Girl, look at you! Look at you! We better find a way to keep the men folk away from your mama, Natra! Lord us plain looking sisters don't stand a chance around her! I cannot wait to see you get out of your car, so I can get the full effect." Natra caught up in Tracey's enthusiasm began stroking Tracey's free flowing, long hairstyle laughed, "Yes mom, you looking good!"

When they arrived at Natra's school, she leaned across the front seat to give her mother a ceremonious kiss (she knew better than actually touch her and mess up her makeup) and a big long hug around Tracey's neck. As they watched, the girl walked toward the school, Nadine noticed two lunch bags on the back seat.

"Well, my good friend Tracey, thanks to the gala affair the girls and I attended yesterday, my daughter's keen sense of giving, and just really good fortune, you will be treated to lunch."

"Why, Thank you," Tracey laughed as the car rattled, rumbled, and banged its way down the street. By the time they arrived at the middle school, Tracey had worked on every nerve Nadine had with her happy, optimistic childlike outlook on life. Several times she wanted to tell Tracey to get real, there really is nothing to be so damned happy about, but like always, she merely listened and nodded. As her car rattled, coughed, and sneezed its way into the parking lot, she saw many of her co-workers on the lot talking, laughing, and apparently enjoying each other.

Vanity never had a better proponent than Nadine. She took a loving glance at herself in the mirror. She exited her car with her usual pomp and ceremony as if a super star. Tracey smiled to herself, while the others complimented, flattered, and praised the hell out of Nadine!

She amiably thanked them as she assured them that she had not done anything special. "Sure!" The females thought as they walked.

Once inside, they were greeted by their principal of five years, the immaculately dressed and pressed Mr. J. Franks - all five feet, four inches of him. For the first day of school, he was sporting a three-pieced white suit, white shirt, white tie, with black and white shoes from the hide of some type of reptile. To some, he looked just like an old Southern Colonel in Black face.

He was as stoic as he was dapper. He instantly changed the mood of most as he dryly reminded them that they needed to be in the auditorium immediately and bolted away. Nadine was convinced he was homosexual as he had never, ever complimented her or even looked at her lustfully. Tracey laughed, while continuing to chirp like a bird.

Someone remarked they certainly did not need air conditioning as long as he was there. They slowly walked toward the auditorium, greeting students and parents along the way.

It became hotter and louder the closer they got to the auditorium. Filled with hundreds of students, parents and other concerned folks, it sounded like a series of sonic booms. All the bedlam promptly ended as Mr. Franks began to address the assembly. He spoke of Black pride, dignity, respect, and the power of knowledge. He languished and was visibly shaken by the knowledge that some of his students had been incarcerated, injured, even killed during the summer. He added that even more had spent the summer idling their time away instead of doing something to enrich their minds and bodies.

"Nothing is wrong with playing hard; however, we need to learn to work hard to earn the privilege of playing hard."

He ended by challenging everybody to begin a year of academic, social, and spiritual excellence. Polite applause. Afterwards, the two vice principals, three counselors, and other assorted school-based dignitaries more or less echoed what the principal had said to an audience that had become extremely restless and bored. It had become hotter, and hotter in the very old auditorium.

Approximately, an hour and half after the principal had spoken, the youngster who had served as master of ceremonies wiped the perspiration from his face while announcing Mrs. Walker would . . . "now introduce the home room teachers of all the students and give further directions."

Nadine had long since acquired a chair and was sitting near the one big, noisy fan in the auditorium. She was completely oblivious to the proceedings until she heard the marvelous sound of her name. With an amiable smile and gestures, she worked the crowd to what amounted to a thunderous ovation. Perhaps the ovation was motivated by the fact they would be leaving the hot, stuffy auditorium and had finished with all those boring speeches.

Feeling remarkable as they cheered, Nadine approached the stage as if she were about to receive an award. Tracey, amused, said softly to herself, "Walk on girlfriend!"

"Good Morning everyone, I am Mrs. Walker, a seventh grade English teacher here at our splendid middle school," she announced with an angelic smile and amiable voice. Nadine paused for additional applause. "It is my job, my responsibility to unite each of you with your brand new home room teachers. I will first call the name of the homeroom teacher, after which I will read the names of the students. Please join your new teacher and move with dispatch with your new teacher to your new homeroom.

"If your name is not called, please stay in your seat until the auditorium is emptied. Then please see one of the counselors. Thank you very much for your time and patience. And have a very great year!"

Nadine cleared the auditorium very rapidly except for the few who had not been assigned. Also, her new homeroom waited for her, some with a great deal of anguish and apprehension, as she was their teacher last year. She looked over the names again, "thirty-seven future doctors, lawyers, or Indian chiefs," she smiled to herself sarcastically. She had known many of them from the prior year and was not too thrilled with the prospect of reliving last year's experiences with them. However, she knew somebody had to pay the bills.

Finally, she led them out of the auditorium up the stairs to her room, her domain, and her principality. The room was decorated with a variety of charts, pictures, photographs, rules, regulations, and other assorted ornaments, which were of minimal interest to the students.

She checked the roll again and was about to tell the class exactly how she wanted things done, when suddenly the halls were full of laughter. Her friend, Tracey, had obviously made another funny and her class was roaring with laughter. It was so infectious that many of hers were laughing, and the others were smiling broadly.

Well, she just was not going to have any of this!

"Ladies and gentlemen," she began with forbidding tone and expression, "this is a school, and you are in a classroom, my classroom. There is a distinct difference between being here and an amusement park. The sooner you learn that fact, the better off we will all be. Nothing has changed since last year. I expect each of you to behave like ladies and gentlemen. I only see one face, (looking directly at Chris) which was not here with me last year. The expectation is that you all will be better this year."

"Still a bitch!" somebody complained softly.

While Mrs. Walker was advising the class of the do's and don'ts in her class, Sonia was gazing out of the window thinking about Roy. She wondered how she was going to deal with his funeral or if she should even go. She began to sob softly as she thought about his gentle smile, his touch, his tender words, and her love for him. Most of the other students were aware of the fact that she and Roy had been lovers.

Many, especially the boys had been fans of Roy. They knew her brother, Little Al, had killed him. Therefore, most were feeling sad and not paying too much attention to Mrs. Walker, but to the softly sobbing Sonia.

Chris could not stand to see Sonia sobbing and turned his head away from her as he felt tears flowing down his face. Others either cried softly or put their heads on the desks to conceal their emotions. Mrs. Walker continued to talk about rules, regulations, notebooks and such. Nadine was unaware of the fact she was talking to herself.

Only Marcus reacted by taking the box of tissue off Mrs. Walker's desk and offering them to Sonia. Sonia managed a little smile, while thanking him. This totally infuriated Mrs. Walker who never liked Sonia as Sonia attracted a lot of attention because she was so irresistible. She did not like Marcus as he was about the ugliest and darkest male she had ever seen.

"Don't you ever touch anything on my desk, you, you . . .!" She began to shriek. Marcus interrupted with his very thick accent, "I'm very apologize deeply, but Sonia is . . ."

Mrs. Walker responded, "I really do not care what Ms. Sonia is, Marcus, you do not under any circumstances . . ."

Another student interrupted, "But Mrs. Walker, you don't understand, Sonia's . . ."

"All I need to understand," Mrs. Walker began harshly, "is that nobody is to touch anything on my desk without my permission. Marcus! You above all should know better. I am sure that in South Africa where you came from, you did not go around taking things. Or did you?"

Prudently, Marcus did not respond. Most stared at her menacingly. Sonia thought about smacking her, but continued to gaze out of the window.

Mrs. Walker took a deep breath, "Now. I want you; class to take out a sheet of notebook paper. I am going to write three suggested topics on the board. I want you to write three paragraphs on any one of the topics."

As she turned to write on the board, a voice yelled, "Forget you, Ms. Streetwalker!"

The class laughed, which infuriated Mrs. Walker!

She pivoted about quickly, and somehow, her eyes focused on Chris whose mouth was wide open. Convinced he was the culprit, she walked directly toward him screaming, "And who are YOU? Talking to, calling me a "Streetwalker?" Have you lost your mind?"

Panicked! Chris jumped up and was about to run, as he was sure this crazy woman was going to beat him up like Dora would.

Sonia yelled, "Leave him alone! He ain't done nothing!"

Mrs. Walker turned to tell Sonia to mind her business, but by now Chris was up and intending to run out of the door.

Quickly, she reached out to grab him! Her long, well-manicured fingernails scratched his face, neck and chest! And she also tore his shirt!

Everything now seemed to stop! And begin again in slow motion. The class was silent for an instant. Mrs. Walker and Chris stood motionless staring at each other for a brief moment.

A voice that sounded like the one who called her the name, defiantly bellowed, "Don't take that shit offa her!" Another, "Call your mama! Get her fired! Sue the bitch!" The young voices began to crescendo, some encouraging Chris to " . . . cancel her!"

The room was suddenly transformed from a class of forty-one students to a mutinous mob of thirty-nine screaming, yelling, and banging on any and everything as Sonia continued to gaze out the window.

They were demanding satisfaction for the unprovoked attack on Chris. The loudest was the little girl in the back of the room. "I hope his mother comes up here and bangs her!"

By now, the bedlam had resounded throughout the old, compact building! Tracey and the other adults including the female vice principal were attempting to control what were now scores of angry, rebellious youngsters from other classes. Many had no idea what had happened but were screaming, yelling, and being generally disorderly.

Mrs. Walker realized she had screwed up, big time! She retreated to the chair behind her desk trying to figure out what to do. By sheer coincidence, she looked up into the face of the little girl in back of the room. As she gazed at her, the girl with a big smile on her face, mouthed, " . . . streetwalker!"

Nadine was now! Painfully aware of the fact that not only had she overreacted, but the child that she grabbed was not the one. Even worse, probably not even a boy.

Tracey was now kneeling in front of her trying to make sense out of the near riot which was now almost under control. To Nadine everything seemed distant and surrealistic.

Frightened and confused she thought, "Maybe before all this is over, I may really have to be a streetwalker."

Chapter 2
Monkey Girl

Mrs. Walker did not even notice that Sonia shot out of the room. She ran down the stairs on a dead mission! Now on the main floor, she saw several students and a few adults crowded around a table manned by Mr. Greene. He had been her counselor last year. She was not sure whether he was still her counselor, but she knew he liked her with his old fresh self! She knew that he would do almost anything she asked as he had always like her mama.

"Hi! Mr. Greene," she began with a big breathless smile.

"Oh, Miss Sonia, you have really grown! You look like you have really been good?" He asked with a broad smile which replaced the beleaguered expression that had been on his face only seconds before.

Checking her out from head to toe he continued, "Have we been Good this summer? Looks like you have really . . .been Good!"

Understanding exactly, what the old man was implying, she faked a little blush and asked as melodiously as she could, "Could I use your telephone? I maybe forgot to lock my door, and I want to call my mother and check. You know she could still be in bed."

Wetting his lips as he visualized Sonia's mama in bed, he was all too willing to help. "Yes, if there is anything else I can . . ." His vision, his focus was broken by some skinny kid asking about a schedule or something.

Once in his office, she called Dora, because she felt Chris needed a little help with that Mrs. Walker whom she did not like anyway! Her big mouth was the reason her brother had been locked up in the first place. She hoped Dora would come up there and total evil assed, big-mouthed Mrs. Walker.

Dora answered the phone as she greedily watched Goldie sample a new supply of coke. The voice on the other end sounded to her like her daughter, Christee. So, predictably, she was annoyed, "The hell you want?"

Sonia was not prepared for that type of greeting and was so startled she started to hang up.

"Dora, uh, Miss Dora. It's me Sonia, and I just called . . ."

Dora quickly collected herself as she recognized the girl's voice. She really liked the idea of having a true admirer like Sonia.

Goldie glared menacingly at Dora as Sonia was telling her about the incident at school. Predictably, Dora had a real fit when told the teacher Had hit and scratched her boy. She thanked Sonia and immediately told Goldie that they had a little business to take care of down at the school.

Goldie's paternal instincts kicked in as she squeezed into her black leather pant's outfit, checked her piece, stuck under her top and was ready to go teacher hunting. Dora cursed, snorted a little more coke, and went into the bathroom to take a shower. Quite a while later, she was also ready to go teacher hunting.

Dressed in an all white, leather jump suit, she looked a lot like a fashion model, which was her one positive quality. She never left the house looking anything but gorgeous. This was the reason that Goldie, her late brother (Rommie), and many others in and out of the life craved her.

"I used to go to this school," Goldie snarled as she parked her late model luxury car in the bus stop. "They used to tease me all the time. Said I lookeded ugly just like a monkey."

Dora glanced at her, smiling and thinking to herself, "Now, you look like an ugly gorilla."

"One day, this boy that I likeded a . . . Why you looking at me like that? " Dora just shrugged.

"Yeah, I used to like boys until . . . well, I liked him enough to buy him a little card, a valentine. My mother helped me to get dressed that morning, and I felt really pretty. I almost ran to school, 'cause this was the day that I was going to get me a boyfriend."

Dora noticed that Goldie was now crying. Goldie was not able to even look at her as she continued; "It was in home room when I went over to him to give him . . . to give him the card. When I handed it to him, he just stood there without saying anything with my red envelope in his hand. The other children started to giggle and laugh! I am embarrassed as hell! Then he said that he did not want a valentine from a monkey girl. He tore it up and threw it in my damned face.

"I leaped on his little ass and started punching him in his face. He fell and I be kicking and stomping him. The other boys and the teacher tried to get me off him, but I was too strong. Then, they were so many of them that they got me off him. They took me down to the principal. I got put out before I could even tell her what happened. She just walked me to the front door and told me not to come back for a week with my mother.

"I sat on the steps and cried and cried. Then, I got mad. I wanted to kill his ass, 'cause they didn't have to tease me, and laugh at me and call me a monkey girl. I, I sneaked back in there. I walked up to the room. They were getting ready to go to another class. There were these old chairs in the hall. I sat in one crying again, trying to think what to do 'cause I really likeded him.

"They came out the room and when they saw me they started calling me 'Monkey girl, Monkey girl'! Somebody pushed him to me. He looked at me and smiled. I thought that he be going to say sorry. He spit on me! He spit on me and be started walking away while everybody was laughing.

"I picked up the chair that I be in and slammed it upside his head! I picked up the broke wood and beat him, and beat him!

The punk was all bloody! And I told him while he was down there not moving that he should not laugh at me and be call me monkey girl.

"His face was all bloody and he was not moving but he lookeded so cute that I bend over and kissed him and told him sorry. They locked me in a closet until the police come and lock me up. They said that I was going to do child life in jail if I be lucky.

"But the judge said I be too sick for that and sent me to this place where they had peoples that be criminal sick. They had me in the women ward. I am the only child in there. There were all kinds of women there done killed they mamas, and cut up they children, burnt up they boyfriends and all kinds of shit!

"That's when them women there straightened me out and I found out that I was supposed to me a man. They teached me how to be a man. Ain't no man ever touched me!"

By this time Goldie was so agitated that Dora was now afraid that she was about to go off!

Goldie sat quietly chewing her tongue for a moment or two. Then she grabbed Dora by her hair, tongue kissed, "Let's get this shit over with! Goldie was visibly shaken as she entered the building with Dora, who was not at this time sure about being in there with Goldie. Dora always knew that Goldie was a little bit off but damn! They walked in and saw a man, Mr. Greene, seated behind the makeshift station she strutted her stuff over to him. While inquiring about her son, she flirted just enough to stimulate the man. However, she was careful not to further annoy Goldie much more. Goldie, who had not been in the building since she had been thrown out so very long ago, was hearing the long departed echoes of the children calling her "Monkey girl".

"Well, let me see," he said smiling at Dora." Yes, there he is, uh, in Mrs. Walker's home room. I am sure that he is still there. It does not look like they have changed any classes yet. Room 201, right ups those stairs to the right. Uh, maybe, after you finish, perhaps I can take you and your, uh, uh, um, (Goldie looked just like something out of a nightmare to him) friend might want to join me for a little lunch or (wetting his lips) something."

Goldie growled, "You little faggot, I buys her 'verthing she wants. He began a weak apology, while Dora blew him a kiss behind Goldie's back, laughing, "You got that right. What in the hell would I want with a broke, drag ass like you? You better take your damned wife to lunch. She's used to cheap shit!"

Dora walked her walk to show the man what he would be missing.

As they walked up the stairs, Goldie confessed to Dora that she did not like the way she flirted. Then she told her that she did not know what she would do if Dora ever left her. She continued by saying that sometimes she could not sleep thinking about her being left for a man. Dora thought, "I'm going to deep six your monkey ass as soon as I can find me a somebody with money, and they were sure right. You do look like a monkey. You are too ugly to be a monkey. You look more like a gorilla!" But she grabbed Goldie by the arm with a reassuring smile, "You know it's you and me!"

Finally, as they reached the room, Dora sauntered in as if she owned the place. The class was stunned as many of them knew her from the neighborhood but never associated her with Chris. The boys carefully watched every movement of Dora as she looked around the room for Chris. Spotting him, she walked deliberately toward him with an expression on her face that frightened him. He wondered what he had done and prepared himself for a beating up by the mistress, Dora.

Surprisingly, she gently asked him to stand as she carefully examined him. Mrs. Walker opened her mouth to say something when she was distracted by the chomp, chomp of Goldie's heavy boots as she menacingly entered the room. The kids who were not particularly fond of their teacher were now scared for her. They knew if Goldie was there, Mrs. Walker just might get blasted!

Nadine's first instinct was to run as she could plainly see that she was in a no win situation. But she knew that her only salvation was to stand her ground; and maybe, she could bluff her way out of it. She managed a smile looking directly at Dora, "Can we? I mean, . . ." She had about lost it!

To add to her discomfort, Goldie was now slowly walking toward her with a grimace on her face. Actually, it was a smile as Goldie found Mrs. Walker exceptionally attractive. Sensing Dora was the least of two evils, she walked in the other direction to face Dora.

"Why you beat up, and scratch up my boy? " Dora began deliberately. "Miss, uh, Mrs. Walker, there has been a terrible mistake and I am sure we . . . that is mature adults can, can come to . . ." Nadine managed.

"Who is this Mrs. Walker you talking at?" Dora snarled!

The pain truth was Nadine was so frightened that she did not even realize that she began to talk before she even knew this woman's name. With pleading eyes, she begged Dora to leave her alone.

Dora knew that look and began to smile, as she knew she had one.

The children also could sense Mrs. Walker was in big trouble and began to crescendo in anticipation of the fight! Chris did not know what to Do. Sonia was now regretting that she had made the telephone call. She felt really ashamed of herself and knew that Roy would not have liked it at all.

Meanwhile, Dora glanced at Goldie who was looking at this woman the way she often caught her lustfully looking at her. Although Dora was convinced she was as fine as a woman could get, she checked this female out from head to toe and had to admit that she was a pretty good-looking woman. Dora liked the way Mrs. Walker looked. She wished she could wear clothes like that. Ironically, Nadine although scared to death, was really impressed by Dora's form fitting, white leather outfit. "Man!" she thought, "I could really, look damned good in something like that! Wonder if she had it made for her?"

The children who were dying to see the two fights disrupted the mutual admiration. The noise in the room drew the attention of everyone on the floor! Students from other rooms began to stampede into the room followed by their teachers who were trying to retrieve them. The excitement and anticipation caused Dora to forget all that stuff about how the woman looked and dressed. It was time to get busy!

Dora screamed a barrage of obscene threats and challenges that stunned Nadine and farther excited the children! Feeding on the energy of the children, she continued to style, profile, and even began playing the dozens! Nadine began to retreat toward her desk where Goldie was now standing. Tracey attempted to come to Nadine's aid; however, she was helpless as she was much too small to force her way though the mass of screaming and clamoring children. Marcus was holding Chris who was close to being hysterical.

Sonia finally realized her adored Dora was a crazy woman. All of the horrible things her mother had said about Dora were true. She felt like crying, crying the bitter tears of disappointment. The little girl who had called Mrs. Walker a streetwalker was totally enjoying the spectacle. Goldie circled the room slowly to get a better view of Mrs. Walker.

This middle school had two advantages over most. These were the two school police, Mr. Maos and Mrs. Parks, who ruled with iron fists to keep everyone safe. Mr. Maos was an awesome, six foot - four, three hundred twelve pounds of muscular no nonsense. He was so large especially to the students that usually all he had to do was to frown and they cowered. Mrs. Parks was a large woman of about five feet seven inches of smiles and hugs who had won a local televised karate contest.

Mr. Maos entered the room and young bodies scattered with remarkable alacrity and dispatch! Mrs. Walker who had never much cared for the man was so happy to see him that she could have kissed him. Even Goldie, who had built her reputation by waxing many men, was fearful. Dora found him attractive and began to turn on the charm. Somehow, the zipper on her top was a bit lower than it had been when he entered.

"What in the world is going on in here, Mrs. Walker? " he bellowed.

Before she could answer, Dora volunteered seductively, "Well, officer, I came up here to see about my boy. That woman beat him up, and I came up here to see about it! It's a damned shame that you can't even send your boy to school these days. You got any children? They as big and strong as you?"

Goldie had eased over to Nadine, grabbed her hand, and stuffed some paper in it. Nadine, concentrating on what Dora was saying, placed what felt like paper in her pocket without really thinking about it.

Not paying too much attention to Dora, he asked Nadine again what had happened. Nervous, she somehow responded that there had been a terrible mistake. To add to her discomfort, Mrs. Parks entered the room.

The sight of the two officers caused Goldie to damn near have a nervous breakdown. It brought back memories of her being taken away by the police long ago. She eased her hand to her piece and leaned on the wall.

Nadine just knew that her career had just flown south.

Dora had begun to pout, as she was not seemingly having the desired impact on the man.

Mr. Maos was anxious to do his duty and arrest Mrs. Walker. Mr. Greene was having a visual feast, comparing Mrs. Walker and Dora.

Mrs. Parker's attention was on Goldie. She recognized her for what she was and did not like her one bit. Mr. Franks exploded into the room! He grabbed Mr. Maos by the arm leading him into a corner, while directing the students to sit and be quiet. With eyes darting around the room, he demanded that Mr. Maos explain what in the world had happened. He hoped the situation did not have to be reported. He was anticipating a promotion and did not want an incident jeopardize it.

Continuing with an excited whisper, "Do you fools know that I was talking to headquarters up when all this started?"

"You know damned well I don't teach these kids! If you want to yell at somebody, you better go to Mrs. Walker! The fool beat up and scratched a kid, and the one in the white came up here to kick her butt! The other one, I suppose, is her back up! I should not say this but, um, don't that other thing look like a monkey or something? (Mr. Franks looked at him blankly as he was not in the mood, even though...) You better go over there and deal with them! Maos retorted, "One more thing, you best watch the way you talk to me! I was doing the job, and maybe if your people did their job . . ."

Mr. Franks' eyes were still darting around the room. He paused, apologized to Mr. Maos with his eyes darting from person to person. But Maos grabbed him by the arm and whispered, "The best thing to do is to arrest Mrs. Walker. You cannot do wrong if she is locked up."

"Locked up Mrs...." He shouted so loudly that he startled the others, especially Mrs. Walker. Then whispering to Maos, "How am I going to look with her last year's Teacher of the Year in this whole damned system locked up? Hell! After she gets locked up, I can kiss any chance of a promotion goodbye. You get out! Take Parker with you. I'll take care of this."

He watched as Maos summoned Parker and with a look of total disdain stormed out of the room. As they departed, Mr. Franks composed himself and walked to the front of the room.

"Well, ladies," he began with his eyes darting from one to another, "we seem to have ourselves a situation that needs a solution that will be fair to all concerned. It has been my experience to, when our youngsters are concerned; find a quick way of resolving a potentially caustic situation. Let's walk down to my office, where we can talk."

In his office, he surveyed his audience. He could sense that Dora, who he hoped was the child's mother, would be easy to deal with. He was right on the money as Dora was now quite bored to death with the whole situation and only wanted to leave. Goldie's only concern was make this sweet thing, the teacher, her lover. Nadine was emotionally exhausted and began to cry softly. She remembered the paper in her pocket and began to wipe her eyes with what she thought may have been tissue. She could not believe her eyes! In her hand were five one hundred dollar bills!

She looked over to Goldie!

Goldie looked her in the eyes and signaled to her to not say anything. Dora saw the look, but thought Goldie was protecting her.

Somehow Nadine found the strength and began, "Mr. Franks and, I am real sorry (looking at Dora), but I, that is, in the confusion, I did not even get your name."

"Dora, everybody calls me Dora!" Dora responded defiantly.

"Well, Miss Dora, there was a terrible accident, and I accidentally tore your son's shirt and there may be a little, uh, scratch. If you, I mean with your permission I will see that he sees the nurse and we can . . ."

"Nurse? If you scratched and beat my boy up and tore his damned clothes off him, you'd damned sight better do better than a damned nurse."

Mr. Franks, seeing an opportunity to bring closure, faced Nadine and asked if she could think of another solution. Nadine promptly suggested that with Dora's permission, she would take the boy to the hospital, have his injuries attended to, and pay for, no, buy him another shirt. Both Mr. Franks and Goldie nodded in agreement. Dora, sick and tired of the whole affair agreed.

The principal sent Mr. Greene to get Chris. While he was gone, the principal dusted off one of his old speeches about folks getting together to overcome any old obstacle. He granted Nadine permission to take the boy to the hospital and a little shopping.

The meeting was now over. Mr. Franks was now alone in his office leaning back in his chair wondering if he had done the right thing.

Chapter 3
Ten Years Older

Sitting in the emergency room with Chris was an educational experience for Nadine. She had been teaching youngsters from the most deprived areas of the city, and she truly knew them. It was her professional and private opinion that they were nothing, and doomed to never, ever be nothing.

Her job was, regardless to what the big shots said, to teach them enough to have language skills to be able to read something of value while they were serving their time in jail, which was inevitable and unavoidable. Or in the case of the girls, they should have enough skills to be able to fill out the welfare forms and to write to their boyfriends in jail.

The fact that she had grown up in similar surroundings had nothing to do with it. She was special, different, and had little memory of being raised in that very same environment herself.

As they left the school, she was determined not to talk to Chris. However, while sitting in the emergency room with him, she found that he was a fascinating boy with a quick and agile mind. Actually, she felt flattered when the receptionist assumed that he was her son and complemented them. She said that he was a good looking young man and looked just like his mother!

As they sat and talked, Chris with his easy manner and smile quickly caused her to be mesmerized by him, and his life down in the country. He told her about this grandparents and the rest of the folks. She recalled and shared some of her fond memories of the South where she, too, had visited relatives. The three hours that they waited melted away. Just before a nurse called them, she felt the need to and apologized to the boy and hugged him. She felt warmness in the hug that was so sincere, so genuine, so open, and so tender that it frightened her. She could not remember any man feeling so warm, so much tenderness as she felt in that hug.

"Man!" She thought, "If you were a few years older, I would be yours."

Things seemed to get better. The doctor assured her that the use of an over the counter ointment would completely clear up the minor scratches. He asked Chris to wait in the waiting room, as he wanted to speak to Mrs. Walker alone. He looked at Nadine as a father would a child who had misbehaved and told her tenderly he would have to file a report.

He told her that teaching was often a thankless low paying profession that caused so much anguish that rage on the part of teachers is more common that one would believe. He continued that she should either seek help or another profession profession. Or maybe, she should go to a church or pray. He assured her everything could work out, but cautioned her to be gentle with the children.

"These youngsters could not choose their parents or their environment, but they do have the potential to serve their God and make a positive contribution to society. Be good to yourself and your family, Mrs. Walker. Take care of and love the children. I never expect to see you here again under these circumstances. May the Lord go with you."

The ride to the shopping center was again very pleasant. It had been the first time she could remember actually enjoying shopping with a child. Chris had been so very appreciative, so amicable and there were no unreasonable demands from him as there usually were with her girls. They had enjoyed lunch together, and Chris kept her in stitches with his quick wit and humor.

Just before reaching his home, she found herself telling him about some of good times she had growing up ". . . right here in these projects... and let me tell you chile, Us were po'!" As they laughed, she entered his parking lot. She watched him walk away from her car with a heavy heart.

She wished her dates had ended the way her day ended with Chris with her wanting more. She laughed, "What dates?" Well, maybe that doctor was right. Maybe the children could amount to something. Maybe it was time for her to be about the business of loving her work and the children.

As she was parking in the nearly empty school lot, she glanced at her watch, 3:24. She stepped out of the car and walked into the building. Still feeling quite good, so good that she spoke to Mr. Maos, which surprised him, as she never, ever spoke to him unless it was official business. She almost skipped up the stairs. She noticed Tracey's light was still on and walked into the room with a big smile on her face. Tracey was glad to see her smiling, but she was very surprised. Tracey like everybody else was very unaccustomed to seeing Nadine in a good mood.

"Girl, what that on your face? Girlfriend, look just like a woman in love?" Tracey giggled.

"What you giggle for, girl?" Nadine matched her poor island accent.

Tracey, now overwhelmed with laughter, "I sure hope you are not having a nervous breakdown, because you is one happy child now. It would be a real sin to waste it!"

"Tracey, I had an incredible afternoon, simply fabulous" she paused and shook her head smiling, "I guess I had a really incredible day!"

"Amen!"

"Stop that, girl! Anyway, My afternoon with Chris was just wonderful! I don't ever remember having so much fun! I could just hug and squeeze him with his little cute self?"

"Little...? Just whom are we talking about wild, and crazy woman?"

Nadine responded teasingly, "You may not have met my little gentleman friend, but I want you to know that he was, like they

26

say, a perfectly great escort and a gentleman. Like I said, if he was mine I'd . . . I don't know what I would have done if Chris were ten years or so older."

Tracey sized up Nadine, "you say ten years older... who is this Chris?"

"The guy, I mean . . . the young man that I took to the hospital."

Totally befuddled, "You mean, this morning you beat up and tore the very shirt off your student. And now you are telling me that you are in love with a, what, twelve maybe thirteen-year-old kid? I was just kidding before, but have you lost your every loving mind?"

"Oh my God!" Nadine shrieked, "Maybe I am losing my mind."

The two looked at each other for a moment and suddenly they both laughed. Nadine told her about the entire experience as Tracey just shook her head in total disbelief. After she finished telling the story, Tracey laughed a nervous laugh and asked how much the clothing cost to change the subject. Nadine reached in her pocketbook and pulled out a handful of assorted bills, which surprised Tracey, because Nadine had complained to her that she just had nine dollars the night before. Johnny had agreed to stop pass his credit union to get some money to lend to Nadine until payday.

Tracey blurted out, "What you do turn a trick with this young gentleman?"

"Oh shit! The money!"

"Money? You talking about the green paper in your hand?"

With a look of near panic, Nadine confided, "Something else happened . . . I need to talk about. I also need a little drink. Will you stop with me? I will not be long. Please say you will. Will you, please?"

"Okay, okay, stop begging, Johnny is going to be late this evening, I'll stop. I will just die if I don't know the rest of what you got yourself into. Just think, last night you were complaining about being so bored. Liked the Good Book says 'be really careful of what you ask for 'cause you just might get it. And tomorrow, I will check out your young gentleman friend."

"Go ahead and make fun of me. I really don't care. Let's get out of here. We can stop at a place that I used to go a little while ago, Eric's. Some fool that I used to go out with took to the place once or twice. It is not that bad and the owner is really fine! They always treated me all right there. That's just what the doctor ordered. Let's go to Eric's."

As they were leaving the school, Mr. Franks was walking toward his car. Both spoke to him. His ever-darting eyes never really focused on either of them. He quickly returned their greeting, jumped into his automobile, and sped away. They two watched him disappear down the street, looked at each other and laughed, Nadine nervously, as she wondered what he was going to do about her.

It was about 4:45 when they entered the club. The music was blasting, and everyone seemed to be having a good time. As her eyes became accustomed to the dim lights, Nadine recognized just about everyone in the place. It was as though she had never left. Many of the men recognized her and began to send the two women drinks. In fact, they were treated to so many drinks that the barmaid joked that they would soon be able to open their own bar.

Along with the drinks, predictably came the men. They would stop; say something really silly or corny, then return to wherever they came from with a sense of accomplishment. They just laughed.

Nadine was drinking a high octane; expensive vodka while Tracey was sipping on a cooler. Nadine was starting to cut loose, while Tracey was wondering why she agreed to come there in the first place. Although a nice bar, it was a bar. She knew that she should stay as far as possible from bars.

Finally, she asked Nadine, "What was it that you wanted to talk about?"

Nadine responded with a blank expression.

"You know, about the money?"

"Damn! You sure know how to spoil a good time!" Nadine laughed as she eye flirted with one of the men.

Nadine, then, told Tracey the whole story from the time that she grabbed Chris through her encounter with Dora and her very funny looking butch friend, Gold something or other, the five hundred dollars, and . . .

"Are you completely out of your damned mind, girl? Do you have any idea, at all, what the hell you are playing with? Any idea at all?"

"What you mean?" Nadine asked as she continued to chain smoke. "What the F.. ! What I mean? You say?" So loudly that the entire bar paused to see what was happening.

"Didn't anybody," Tracey continued, "ever tell you about taking stuff, especially money from a stranger?"

"Yeah, but this was different, because I really needed some money."

"Of all the dumb stuff I have known you to do this has got to be . . ."

Nadine impatiently, "the hell she going kill me for a lousy five hand . . .?"

Nadine thought about her predicament and became very scared. There was an expression of eminent concern on her face. She blurted, "W-What in the hell was I thinking about?"

Tracey felt this was a good time to calm her friend down, rather than, to chastise her. "Girl, maybe Somebody is trying to tell you something."

"Now, no preaching Tracey," as she took another gulp.

"I know better than trying to get you to do something that you don't want to do. Now, I've heard you talk about the fact that your mother did not understand you, but I only wished that I had one parent that cared enough for me to not understand me. Both of my folks were street people, big time. They both spent as much time as they could bar hopping and partying. They both had what we politely call extra marital affairs.

"They both were whores and neither allowed anything to keep them out of the streets. My folks had sort of a competition. Every time one got somebody new, the other had to get one just a little bit better. And me, they used me as the judge. One would take me out with their new one, and the other would ask me about the person. Then the other would do the same thing. By the time I was twelve or thirteen, I had more aunts and uncles than the legal law allows, you know, what they call open relationships today.

"Well, as you could imagine, I could do anything that I wanted. I started smoking and drinking when I was about ten or eleven. Sex, Hell, I had my third abortion when I was fourteen. But you know, my parents were both spoiled kids playing at being adults, parents, and they both were prominent people. Prominent in their professional lives, had all the political connections, and they were prominent in the church."

Tracey was interrupted by the bar maid bringing them more drinks from the men in the bar. Nadine smiled thanks as Tracey continued, "You know, sometimes God is getting into your life, and you just don't realize it. Anyway, Aunt somebody was sitting in her long, candy red Caddie in front of our home when I came home from that private school that they shipped me off to I got off the bus and ran toward the house."

Nadine was drinking heavily but hanging onto every word. Tracey paused every once and awhile to make sure that she was not talking to herself.

"Well, as I was running to the house, my father was calmly strolling by me with a couple of suit cases. Then, he turned to me and held out his arms to hug me. I loved my daddy. He was so big, strong, and so smart. He was one of the few successful Black lawyers at that time. So, I ran to him, and we hugged. I ain't seen that man for almost ten years. He and that blond" aunt "just went that day and never to be seen by me again. I got a drawer full of checks that he has sent me. Never came to see me do anything. Just gone, graduations, nothing, just gone!

"Then my mother had her turn at making me feel like shit. She always blamed me for his leaving. So, we were two hens living together. My mother never hit me or abused me physically, but she really did a job on my head. Now that Daddy was gone, we started competing for the attention of men. Sick!"

"You and your mother were seeing the same men?"

"Not then, I mean, right after Daddy left she started having them uncles come to the house. Now, at first she would introduce me to them, but if they even complimented me their asses were history with my mother. After a few incidents like that she stopped introducing me. The buzz words were that I'm going to have company tonight." That meant that I was to stay out of sight. But when a boy came to see me, she would prance around half nude, you know, the teasing ... the only time that I would bring them home was when she was not. "But we kept our front up in church. Our family grew a bit as some of the good church folk found out my daddy was gone. The deacons joined the uncle's parade. Well, about two, three years and a few more abortions later, my mother, and I started hunting the same game. My father would send her money, but she did not want it. So, there I was with more money than any child should have. We, I, could buy anything that I wanted, go any place I wanted, with whomever I wanted. You could not tell me anything. It was a real miracle that I graduated from high school, but not really; because my mother was tough!"

"She had all of them? Your mother is some kind of doctor, isn't she?"

"Yeah! And she has slept her way onto every important board in the state." Tracey nervously laughed, "maybe the whole country? Anyway, the kids at school were a real bore, I out dressed everybody including the teachers. I had the newest car in school, a real slick convertible, and pockets full of money.

"Soon, I whored my way up and down the social scale. I had men who were doctors, lawyers, athletes, and drug dealers, just about anyone with pants sniffing after my hot butt! I was having a ball but at the same time I was lonely. The older I grew, the more I was being used. Used by Satan! I can remember at nineteen, before I went to college making car payments for this guy that I was in love with. I bet I gave him the best fifteen seconds of my life. "

Nadine's high-octane drinks were really beginning to kick in!

"W- w-what then ?" she stammered.

"By the time I was twenty, I was almost completely burnt out. I had abused my body to the extent that, well, I was pretty well used up! My mother was getting a bit tired of her friends asking her about what college I was going to. So, the next thing I know my hot butt was on the campus of the state university. I really don't think that through all this I was really a bad girl, although I did a lot of bad things. I was out there; but even though my flesh was weak, regardless to what I did I kept on praying to God for forgiveness. That was really important to me."

"You were doing all that and praying? Why ?"

"Somehow, it was important to me."

Nadine began to total another drink, "Well, here's to ya! What else happened, Miss Hot Pants."

Undaunted Tracey continued, "I believe, no I know that God was looking out for me whenever I was not looking out for myself. I believe that I was pissing off the devil, because although I was seduced with money, infamy, drugs, men, and what have you, I kept on praying. Now, when that did not work, he started to work on my vanity. He caused me to be ill. The fast life had kicked my butt. My doctor kept fussing with me, because he said that I had a forty or fifty year old body at twenty-one. So, I paid him no attention. I just found me a quack that told me just what I wanted to hear.

"I was invited to a Halloween party at a ski lodge. I went and dressed like a stripper. I drank too much, snorted too much of that coke, and decided to drink a bottle of champagne in the outdoor hot tub. I passed out in it. My escort had found another to sleep with that night and everybody else was partying and forgot all about me. I fell asleep outdoors in the tub in the cold and it started snowing really hard. Then the devil tried to end it all while he had me. Somebody saw me, but they could not wake me up. I went back and forth between life and death several times in the hospital. I..."

Suddenly, Nadine turned green! She jumped up and ran to the rest room. Tracey knew that move as she had made it and seen it countless times. She followed her into the room. By the time she got there, Nadine had expelled much of her high-octane fuel. Tracey urged Nadine to leave the place, get something to eat, and go home to sleep it off. Nadine agreed, but asked her to go to the table and wait while she got herself together.

Sitting at the table alone, she continued to think about her life and near early death. Sipping on her drink, she recalled her unconscientious vision. It seemed that her grandmother who had died when she was a very small child met her in an all white room. Her grandmother smiled at first, then told her that she would be returning to the living world, but she had to do better.

She continued by saying that soon she would find true love and something to do with her life that would be very important. Her granny kissed her, and asked to do better when she got back. She remembered promising her grandmother that she would, and she was revived She was determined to do better as her grandmother asked.

When she got back to school, she studied and worked very hard to be the type of person that her grandmother would be proud of. Everything was fine until an old friend unexpectedly came to the campus to see her. She really cared for and was very happy to see him. He told her that he was starting to get it together and maybe they could start something serious.

They went partying to celebrate at one of her friend's home. He was totally turned off as she drank too much and snorted too much coke. He met and began spending his time with another female. Agitated and behaving like her old spoiled self, she jumped into her car and sped away. Racing down the highway, she passed out and crashed. Again, she was near death.

Some guy asking her if she wanted to dance. She politely declined and looked around the bar. In the middle of the floor was Nadine dancing with a couple of guys. Although fast, the dance motions were extremely suggestive and she was obviously ripped. Tracey did not like the way the guys were touching her friend. So, she went over and escorted Nadine from the dance floor. Nadine sat down for a moment and started gulping down another one of the free drinks. One of the vultures who had been dancing with her came over to the table to fetch Nadine. Tracey intervened and declined his offer to dance with Nadine.

The guy became agitated with Tracey, and asked Nadine ". . . this bitch you Mama or something? I didn't ask her shit! I want you with your fine self."

"No, she ain't my Mama, fool! She just came in here with me."

Tracey was feeling that warm feeling that one experiences when one does something for a friend and they really appreciate it. Nadine gulped down some more of the fuel and continued, "I do just what the hell I want! And I want to dance with you . . . Come on! She's just somebody that I work with!"

Then, she turned to Tracey with a defiant expression, "Why don't you go home to Johnny? You scared that he ain't home?"

Tracey stood up as her former friend walked towards the dance floor.

She walked out the door misty eyed as she knew that Nadine was on her way to the bottom. Thinking about her own life, she realized that sometimes one has to hit rock bottom in order to get it together. She said a quick prayer for Nadine as she walked down the street hunting for a cab.

The cab driver blessed her very soul out! He told her that she had no business in that neighborhood that time in the evening. He was just furious; especially, when she told him that she was married and a teacher. She knew that he was absolutely correct.

During the ride home, she continued to think about her second encounter with death. While she was clinically dead, she again saw her grandmother. She did not seem to be very upset with Tracey; in fact, she just beamed as she said, "Girl what are we ever going to do with you? You know most people only get one chance to cross over, and your total will be maybe four."

They were now standing in a beautiful garden. The greenery, the flowers, and the aromas were far beyond her ability to describe. Her grandmother, still smiling, said to her, "Now, sweetheart what you need is a dream. You need to find something to do with that marvelous brain and other talents that you possess to help somebody else. You must find a way to make us proud of you."

There seemed to be other things that happened, but she could not recall what they were. However, when she became conscience, she just knew that she had to be a teacher. A teacher in the city, which was near the university, would be perfect for her. She realized that she had misused her body, so she began to diet and exercise. She realized that she had misused her mind, so she began to soak up all the knowledge that she could like a sponge. More, importantly, she realized that she had neglected her God, so she joined and became very active in an inner city church with a young, dynamic minister, Michael Govans.

She and her husband, Johnny were very active members of his church. Her thoughts were interrupted by the cab driver asking, "Is this where you live?"

"Yes, sir. You could have taken me to Chicago. I was not paying any attention at all."

They both laughed.

She thanked, paid him, and smiling kissed him on the cheek for really caring. They exchanged blessings, and he stayed for a moment to be sure that she got into her home safely before he drove away. On his way from her home, he wondered why he happened to be in the neighborhood where he had picked her up. He had no fare in his cab, and he always tried to avoid that area like the plague. He shook his head and began to hum a hymn as he drove away.

As she entered her home, she could smell aromas temptingly oozing from the kitchen. Johnny was standing in the kitchen doorway just a smiling. She dropped everything, ran to him, kisses and hugged him! While he stood there motionless wondering what had come over her. She kissed him again and again, and with loving tears exclaimed to the top of her voice, "I love you."

He laughed the laugh of a very happy man.

Chapter 4
Friends

Johnny gently guided Tracey to the kitchen table and began serving her the meal that he had prepared. Johnny continuously shook his head as Tracey told him about the unbelievable things that had happened at school. His eyes revealed concern as she continued by telling him that Nadine wanted to talk. She continued by telling him that Nadine invited her to go to a bar. He knew that his wife did not like the bar scene as she very seldom drank.

She started sobbing softly as she told him about the way she had been treated by Nadine in the bar. She tearfully declared that she and Nadine could never be friends again. He looked at her lovingly and could feel her pain.

"You know," he began, "this life is very strange. You go about your life, having a good time then all of a sudden it happens. From nowhere comes a stumbling block or two, sometimes instead of a block, it is a whole mountain comes crashing down on you. Tracey managed to smile. Anyway, we wonder why those we love betray us. Does it mean that we have loved the wrong people, or maybe, is love wrong?"

"No," she responded softly.

"Perhaps it means that we are called upon to help folks who do not seem to want or even deserve our love, friendship, or certainly not our help. I guess that these are times that we really need to search our souls for guidance."

"Guidance?" She replied softly, talking more to herself than her husband.

"Yes, guidance." he responded.

"Well, all I was trying to do was to be her friend and she just shit all over me! It is not fair and I will not stand for it!" She screamed.

Johnny watched his wife jump from the table screaming with tears flowing. Totally frustrated, she picked up a glass and slammed it on the floor! She glared at him as if he were the very devil as she picked up the plate that she had been using and threatened to smash it.

"Go ahead and break it, if that's what you what to do," he said softly. "If it will make you feel better total all of them."

She stood in the middle of the kitchen not really knowing what to do.

Johnny opened his mouth to say something but decided against it. Tracey ran from the room crying. He could hear her running up the stairs. He took a deep breath while walking toward the closet, where he retrieved the broom and began to sweep up the broken glass. Afterwards he cleaned up the kitchen while trying to figure out what he was going to say to his wife. He could hear her fumbling around in the bedroom.

Just as he finished washing the dishes, he could hear the sound of the shower. He ran up the stairs into the bathroom where she was about to step into the shower. Johnny looked at Tracey saying to her softly. "You know that whatever happens to you out there, I love you and I'm always here for you."

"Johnny, I'm so sor . . ."

"Don't you ever tell me that," he interrupted smiling, "you just get started while I snatch these clothes off and join you. We got to save money you know. Two can shower cheaper than one."

"Hurry! Before I get cold."

Meanwhile, back at the bar, Nadine had guzzled up enough of the "do it fluid" that she had long lost her inhibitions and was acting like an animal in heat. Men were jockeying and maneuvering themselves; so that, they could be the one who would take her away and service her and her hot self.

She staggered to the bar to get another drink. Virginia refused to serve her. Nadine began to cuss and fuss. The vultures insisted that she could drink all she wanted. Eric intervened and diplomatically suggested that she had enough.

Seizing the opportunity, one vulture, grabbed her gently by the arm and told her that he would take her to a place where she could drink all she wanted. Virginia looked at Eric with an anxious expression. Eric took a deep breath and persuaded the guy to back off. While he was talking, Nadine began to feel very sick. She ran toward the rest room! Eric gestured to Virginia to follow her. The vulture watched and casually said to Eric, "Yeah, you right, who the hell want some old drunk . . ."

"Sure you right," Eric responded as he walked behind the bar to serve a customer.

After about five minutes or so, Virginia came back to her station. She remarked to Eric that she was glad that she wasn't going to be that woman's head in the morning. Eric grunted.

Finally, Nadine came out of the rest room and somehow managed to get to and sit on a stool. A guy slammed her pocketbook in front of her. She managed a very weak 'thank you'. Virginia fixed her a seltzer while gazing at Eric.

Eric looked at the woman carefully and seemed to remember her.

He seemed to recall that she was a social worker, teacher or something, but was not really sure. Whatever, he knew that she was in no shape to get home alone. He walked over and asked her whether there was someone who could pick her up. She thanked him meekly but said that she could drive home. Disquieted, he suggested that she catch a cab and get her car in the morning. She thanked him for his concern but insisted on driving herself.

Concerned for her safety and his liquor license, he asked her if she drank coffee. She nodded. " Well, I tell you what, our kitchen is closed. I was about to fix myself a pot. Would you care to join me?"

"I don't want to impose or cause you any trouble," she responded with a beleaguered smile, "but I could sure use a cup about now."

He escorted her to the kitchen as the male customers remarked sarcastically that it must be real 'nice' to own a bar. He ignored them as they walked pass them. Once in the kitchen, the two struck up a conversation as they waited for the water to boil. He asked her if she had ever stopped there before, as he seemed to remember her. She laughed and replied that she had dated a guy who brought her there a few times. Eric was beginning to feel that she was not that bad after all. She sure was an attractive woman.

As they finished their second, maybe third cup, she felt relaxed enough to tell him that she was a divorced woman, teacher, and mother of twin teenaged girls. He laughed saying that none of those things qualified her for the gas chamber. Both laughed as she began to really check him out. "I could really go for this guy," she thought.

Nadine felt so very comfortable that she told him about her day. After she finished, he asked her why she took the money. She replied that she just was not thinking and could not see any harm in it. "What a fool!" he thought as he told her that he really had to get back to his business. She recognized by his abrupt change of enthusiasm that she should have kept that information to herself. He escorted her back to the bar where she told him that she felt much better and could drive home. He nodded politely and walked away. She gave the barmaid a twenty, thanking her for her kindness as she slowly walked out the door to her car. For once, it started without the usual temper tantrums.

As she drove home, she could not help to think of how inconsiderate Eric had been. "Tell them that you maybe made a little mistake, and they don't want to have anything to do with you. Just like a man."

Tracey and Johnny had long since completed their shower and were lying in bed still under the spell of the romantic experience that they had shared. Snuggled in his arms, she asked him if he thought that she had overreacted to Nadine. He squeezed her, kissed her and replied, "Maybe."

"Maybe?" she screeched as she was expecting a different reply.

"Listen, Baby, I cannot tell you who to like and to dislike. I certainly cannot tell you to even speak to Nadine if you choose not to, but I can remember a cute little scared woman at a traffic light. She was sitting in her car in one of our city's worse corners, battling herself and the devil. She was being tempted to do drugs again, but something kept her from making the buy.

"Along came this very nosey police officer in his patrol car and notice this cute, young woman sitting there. He thought that she was a child, maybe, in a stolen car. She looked too young to be driving. (Tracey blushed.) So, he stopped and asked her for her license. Although she was very nervous, she had the prettiest smile. Right then and there, that bad old cop knew that he was in love.

"It was one of those moments that poets write about, and the cop and the lady felt that special something. That night she said something to him that changed that old cop's bachelor life forever.

"She told me about her near death experiences. I can hear you, sweetheart, just like it was yesterday. You said that the devil tried to seduce me with money as you parents had plenty. You said your grandmother had taught me about His love. He tried to make you bitter by giving you parents who were so self-centered that they paid little attention to you. When that did not work, he tried to take your self-esteem. Even being introduced to drugs. You never lost sight of your God"

They embraced, kissed, and cried tears of happiness, thanksgiving, and joy. "So, tell me that with all that He has brought you though, you want to forsake your friend when she is in so much need. Is that really what you want to do?"

"Johnny, how can a man as wise as you waste your time being a cop? You need to go to school and be a man of the cloth. I bet you would give Reverend Govens a run for his money with your fine self."

He smiled as he grabbed her with one hand and turned out the light with the other. The room was instantly filled with ecstasy.

By this time, Nadine had arrived at her home. She was mentally, and physically exhausted as she entered the living room where her daughters were to nose fussing and cussing at each other. Nadine thought that she heard Natra call Shala some kind of whore but really hoped not. Given their history, if one had called the other a 'whore', it was likely to have been Shala to Natasha too tired to deal with it and was about to just go upstairs and drop dead sleep.

Natra gazed at her mother with a look of nullification on her face, "It is, what, eleven thirty and you bounce in here all late. I don't know about fish face here, but I'm hungry. Ain't nothing in the 'fridge and you come in here like some old . . ."

"Look, child, I'm your mother and regardless to what you think, I will not have no child of mine talk to me like that."

Uncharacteristically, Shala agreed by saying softly almost meekly, "I am a little hungry, too."

Nadine felt like just walking out and never returning. She felt that everything was going wrong. Was she the blame? She dug in the purse, and pulled out a couple twenties. She walked toward the girls and handed each one. Nadine made herself smile as she told them to order themselves a pizza or something. Both were shocked, as they could not figure out where she got the money.

"You seen Daddy?" Natra volunteered.

"No, just call for some pizzas, I know that you are going to need two," she said almost sarcastically. Nadine turned and walked up the stairs, while her, now, stunned daughters watched her in disbelief.

"Where did she get money?" Natra asked.

"Who cares, I'm gonna order." Shala replied.

Too though, Nadine was now in her room throwing her cloths in the chair. She took a long look at herself in the mirror. "I took a licking today, but I keep on ticking," she lamented.

Returning from the bathroom, she checked her telephone for messages. A salesman, a bill collector, that fool mechanic, and then what sounded like a very exasperated and furious man screaming, "You dirty bitch, my wife found that little surprise that you left in the car today. Why did you do it? Answer the telephone yourself! I'm tired of talking to your sister! Just tell me why. Your sister can't do it. After all the shit we've done, all I did was take you home and you . . ."

Nadine was furious with Natra as she listened to the next message, "Now nobody's gonna answer the phone! This ain't no game, bitch." The next message, "Look, Shala, please talk to me. I am sorry for screaming at you. All I want to know is why you did that to me. Look it's about nine thirty . . . I will call back about ten, please talk to me. Maybe we can work this thing out, somehow."

"Shala?" She played back the message. Sure enough, it was Shala. The next message, "Nadine, how was your first day back with the kids? Bet you really had fun. Listen, we would like to take the twins shopping this weekend. I'll call tomorrow to see if it is all right. Bye." The next message, (that mysterious male voice again, But this time pensive.) "Shala please talk to me. Looks like I'm going to be single real soon. Please, I'll call you back."

"Shala" she whispered to herself in total denial. She loved Natra all right, but she reminded her too much of their father. Shala, on the other hand was her heart and soul.

"Shala," she moaned, "what in the world have you gotten yourself into?"

The half-closed door opened while a jovial voice asked, "Mama, you want a slice of pizza? Here's a slice."

"Shala?"

"No, mama, it's me."

Nadine collapsed back on the bed, trying to figure out what to do about her other daughter. Natra could see the concern on her mother's face and sat on the bed besides her offering her the slice of pizza. "What's wrong?"

Helplessly, Nadine responded by asking what her sister had gotten herself into. The girl looked at her distressed mother, shrugged her shoulders, suggesting that she talk to Shala. Nadine accepted the pizza and began eating it. She stood up from the bed. She paced aimlessly around the room. Seeing her mother preoccupied, she said, "I'll be in my room."

Nadine did not notice her leaving the room.

On her way to her room, a very exasperated Natra moaned, "I am sure tired of covering for old fish face."

Mind made up, Nadine stormed downstairs. Much to her chagrin, Shala was in the midst of doing some kind of exotic dance with her eyes closed, opened them. Seeing her mother, knowing that she was cold busted by the look on her mother's face glared at Nadine defiantly.

"Who is the man on the phone? What you crazy?" Nadine demanded.

"What guy?"

"Don't, don't fool with me, Shala! Who is this man and what did you do?"

Shala more aggressively, "I don't know what you are talking about! Probably some lie that Natra done told you!"

"No! Baby! Natra would not talk to me about whatever you are doing. It is on the damned phone, my damned phone!"

Knowing for sure that she was cold busted, Shala ran up the stairs, screaming, "I hate you! I HATE EVERYBODY! WISH I WAS DEAD!" She ran into her room, slammed and locked her door. Nadine slid on the couch wondering what to do.

"This is too damned much! I should just get dressed and jump in that old assed car and drive away. I'm tired of being a mother, teacher, and all things people want me to be twenty - four hours a day, seven days a week."

At that same time Mr. J. Franks was finishing a late dinner with his wife. She listened carefully as he told her about the incident with Ms. Walker. He concluded, "Somebody is going to have to pay the devil if this thing gets out. I would sure hate to lose her, because she's a good teacher. One of the most egotistical people I have ever met, but a damned good teacher."

His wife without the least bit of hesitation demanded, "After you finish, get yourself a drink and write exactly what you know about this unfortunate situation. Tomorrow you let Maos do his job. If somebody has got to pay, let it be her. You did not attack the kid, she did. I'll make a couple of calls tomorrow to be sure that your butt is covered. We have worked too hard for this to mess up our plans."

"You are right. I will get right on it."

Chapter 5
Precocious

Morning came much too slowly for the overanxious Chris who had hoped and prayed for this day since he'd been in this big stinking city, the very first day of school! With all their might, the moon and the stars held back the sun, as he just could not sleep. He was not sure what the first day would be like but he was ready.

The second hand on his clock moved so slowly and loudly that he was out of bed, showered and dressed before it moved. Chris inhaled some cereal as he was much too hyped to cook anything. He was not hungry, but needed something to do. Chris checked himself in the mirror at least a million times to make sure he had just the right look. He opened the front door to let the cool early morning breeze fill the living room.

The lazy, hazy morning sun found Chris on the couch trying to watch the early morning news. Soon, Chris was in a very deep sleep. Later when Marcus came to get him, he was for real knocked out.

"Chris!" Marcus called through the screen door, "you alright? What's wrong with you?"

Chris woke up in a cold sweat. He looked at Marcus and began to mumble, "I was dreaming…" Chris decided not to tell him about his dream. He had dreamed that he had gone to school and was attacked by some kind of strange female-like monster with long claws! In his dream, he could not get away! Lord, there was

46

no way he was going to tell Marcus about it. Marcus was about the only friend Chris had and he didn't want him to think he was crazy.

So, he managed a big smile, "... we are going to have a great day."

He knocked on Dora's bedroom door to give her a chance to fuss over him and Marcus on their first day of school. Looking somewhat like the monster in his dream, Dora entered the living room and greeted them by dryly asking if they had breakfast (not that she had any intention of preparing them any). Marcus thanked her saying that he had already eaten with his grandfather. Chris replied by saying that he had only called to tell her that he was leaving.

Dora looked at Chris carefully and asked him to wait for a moment as she walked back to her bedroom. She returned handing him and Marcus each five dollars for lunch. She looked at the pair again, yawned and walked back to her room without saying another word.

Chris said inaudibly to the closing door, "I'll really like school." Marcus took a deep breath and said, "Well we'd better leave. We do not want to be late on our first day."

They had the tools to beat ignorance into submission. Their arsenal included the pens, pencils, and notebook with paper waiting for the storage of wisdom. Just as they were about to turn the corner, they heard Sonia call out to them. Nothing could have prepared them for Sonia. She looked more like a young girl than the temptress. Nothing could be done to hide her well- developed body, but she looked very different without the makeup. Without it, she looked about innocent and pretty to Marcus. Her greeting lacked her usual zestful enthusiasm that made her seem old and detached. She was like a flat warm cola on a hot day. It also surprised Marcus, as last year she never brought books. She said books made her look like a rookie.

And, she was on time. Sonia never seemed to get to school before ten. Given their past, she was amazingly gracious, even asking the boys if they minded if she walked with them. Marcus had been her target since he arrived from South Africa. She was the one who gave him his nickname "jungle bogga" which instantly stuck with the kids at school. However, all this made Chris feel a little sad as she appeared almost completely out of it. The sounds of their tennis shoes on the sidewalk made more noise than they did as they continued toward school.

As they passed the basketball court, she could not bear to even look in that direction. Sonia cringed as she heard a ball bounce on the court. She glanced back to see if Roy were there. Chris turned his head away as he thought he was going to cry. Marcus wanted to hug his former tormenter and tell her things would work out. However, the three walked silently toward school.

Never when he lived in Georgia did he even imagine that there were as many kids as there were in the school's hot, very hot auditorium. Mixed in the total mayhem were cussing, fussing, screaming, singing, rapping, greetings, and name calling. He felt bad for his friend who was being jeered and called jungle bogga. Sonia instantly became a target. They could hear the loud whispers and jeers of some of the students, mostly girls. Her crazy brother killing Roy was common knowledge.

As rare as ice water in hell was sympathy for Sonia. A girl sitting right behind her with her posse bellowed, "My mother say he got just what he deserved for messing with that skunky girl. She going around acting like she a grown up ho and him like ain't no women his age. She says she sorry he had to die like that and all, but that kinda shit happens when people act like that."

The closest thing to support heard was a boy saying that his mother said that everybody needed to mind their own business and leave others alone. None of these had any effect on Sonia as she was deeply absorbed by her own private hell.

The principal immediately caught Chris' attention with his all-white attire. Mr. Franks reminded him of old Col. G.W. Lee back in Georgia. G.W.'s family was one of the oldest plantation owning families in the South. They said that his great, grand daddy was a civil war colonel. Anyway, Chris watched Mr. Franks quiet the chaos and talk forever just like ole G.W. would have. Marcus had never been impressed by any of the activities in the auditorium and this was no exception.

The auditorium had always been a big torture chamber for Marcus. The noise, the smells of the unwashed mixed with cheap perfumes and other stuff meant to be sweet along with the jungle bogga taunts made it almost unbearable. Outwardly, he seemed fine but it really hurt. He was anxious to get to the books where he always did better than his tormentors.

His final report card had been excellent except for the modest grade given to him by Mrs. Walker. His grandfather had spoken to Mrs. Walker and Mr. Franks about his grades that did little good as she argued that his spoken language still needed a lot of hard work. After these conferences Jacque reminded Marcus to expect the world to be unfair. After his final report card, Jacque laughed, telling the boy it would be unlikely that he would ever be in Mrs. Walker's class again in life but there he sat.

Sonia's night had been an emotional roller coaster. First, she relived her last happy moments with Roy. Sonia felt the eagerness she experienced, as she and Roy were about to go make love. She could see his face, even his lips moving, but could not hear him. She could see Roy approach them with that demonic scowl. She wished that she and Roy could fly away.

She could see her hand waving goodbye to Roy who looked real scared. He seemed to be begging her not to leave him, but she could not understand what he was saying as there was laughter drowning out his voice. As she floated away, she looked at her brother's huge hands that were bloody. Then she could clearly hear Roy's terrified voice telling her that he was being killed. She woke up trembling, wanting to but unable to scream. Her dolls watched anxiously but were unable to help. Sonia, now, could not trust her sleep. She sat up in her bed, gazing into oblivion.

In there, she found a memory of her being held and kissed by Roy with what he denied were tears in his eyes. He whispered,

"Sonia, you are truly the most wonderful woman I could imagine. Look at you with your smooth skin, dancing eyes, beautiful, and built like a brick you know what and to top all that you are very precocious. I wish we could spend the rest of our lives together forever alone starting right now."

She recalled asking him what that "p" word meant. She recalled him telling her that it meant in her case, gifted and talented. He ended by saying that they both were and really should stay away from each other for a while, a long while. But then he kissed her and it was on!

About this time, Virginia had returned from work and went directly to Sonia's room. When see looked in the girl's room, she was sitting up in her bed with her eyes wide open but expressionless. Virginia slowly walked to the foot of the bed to get a better look at her. She softly called Sonia. She immediately responded by crying. This relieved Virginia's fear.

Sonia jumped up in the bed and just about knocked her mother down! As they bounced off the dresser, a picture of Sonia and Roy crashed to the floor. Their eyes followed it to the floor, then to each other. Seeing the anguish in the girl's eyes, Virginia assured her that they would be strong together. She told Sonia that all she has heard were good things about Roy. She continued by saying she wished she had met the boy.

"Sonia, even though I did not approve of you two being together like that, nothing, I mean nothing makes what L.A. did right. I mean as his mother I feel some responsibility for what happened. By my son's hands your Roy died."

This statement bewildered Sonia so much that all she could manage was a tearful, "oh mommy." After some hugs and tears, Virginia told her that she didn't have to go to school if she really did not feel like it, but Sonia really wanted to go.

"We always hurt when those we love die, and I know the way Roy died makes it harder to understand. I know you feel kind of guilty, because you left him with your brother. How were you to know, I mean L.A. is a very sick person? Right now he does not know who or what he is.

Again they cried together. Virginia tucked Sonia in bed with a tender kiss and prayer. Soon Sonia was soundly asleep.

Chris watched anxiously as the crowd in the auditorium thinned out with their new classes. Soon he would be with his new classmates with a chance to make new friends. This would make his staying in this big old city worthwhile. He got much more than he had hoped, as Sonia and Marcus would be in his class. To make matters better, the lovely lady who had been in charge was to be his homeroom and first period English teacher. Man was this going to be a great school year!

In the classroom, Chris was not aware of much that was going on. He had become so infatuated with this sensational woman that he was daydreaming that they were off somewhere with her fussing over him. He heard a girl behind him yell out something! He involuntarily opened his mouth as Mrs. Walker suddenly spun around looking directly at him! He was shocked when this woman's face turned blood red as she accused him of something. Her arm looked like one of those tractor arms as it reached for him. The monster! He jumped up to run, but stopped as he felt a sharp pain on his face and heard his new shirt tear.

The rest of the time was a vague impression to him. Everything happened so fast that it was difficult for his mind to keep up! Just as things were starting to make sense to him, Dora and Goldie walked in the door. His nerves were just about shot and stayed that way until he was alone with Mrs. Walker in her car.

Now in his bed, about sleep, he knew for sure that he was in love with Mrs. Walker.

That evening before that first day of school had been one of surprise, discovery, and joy for Marcus. His grandfather had received some wonderful news. He had received a letter from the insurance company that had insured his parents and were making a huge offer for settlement. They had finally received death certificates from the South African government. He would meet with them soon to discuss the offer.

The money would be enough for them to stop existing and start living. There would be much better schools, much less noise and violence, and more important, a place of their own. With tears in his eyes, he explained to Marcus that sometimes-in life a little bit of good can come from a tragedy.

They celebrated by going to a good old soul food pig out joint. While there, Marcus was told about some of the silly and cute things his mother had done as a child. Jacque shared some things that he had all but forgotten. As they left to go home, they felt closer than ever before.

When they arrived home, Jacque told Marcus to have a seat and hurried off to get a forgotten treasure. He searched until he found an old worn notebook. It contained some poetry and stories his daughter had written. Jacque told him to read a story his mother had written when she was about his age. Her story was about a Black knight who searched the world for truth. The brave knight had adventures with all kinds of strange creatures. One day he met a pretty young princess who had to straighten her hair, because it was not long and straight, silky like the ones in the books.

"You take this and read it," Jacque began beaming with pride, "it was like your mother knew she was going to meet and fall in love with your father."

Marcus read the short story repeatedly and loved the way it ended along with the other poems and stories. It read, "...although their work on earth was not done, they went on to the great forever to fight for right and truth."

After reading the story, Marcus now felt much better about the death of his parents. Things had changed radically in South Africa as his grandfather predicted. He was proud that his parents had sacrificed themselves so many others could live in peace and harmony. Marcus' prayer had been for years that he could cry. He cried with pride.

He was delighted when the first day ended. The circumstances of the morning had kept him from sharing with Chris that morning. Now that Chris had left, he would have to wait to talk to him. Marcus felt a sudden surge of energy as he walked away from school.

He walked around to the side of the school where there was a badly kept athletic field with a track. Marcus set his books down and began running around the track. He ran like the wind!

Soon he felt the eyes of his parents looking down on him smiling. His tall, lean frame soared around the track like a low flying eagle. The perspiration on his ebony skin made him look like a god.

Sonia was late leaving the building and saw Marcus running around the track. She cleared herself a space and sat in the empty stands. Her heart pounded excitedly as she watched him. She regretted ever calling him jungle bogga as she now saw he was kind of cute.

As Marcus glided pass the stands he saw Sonia, which made him happy. Excited, he picked up his pace, but she was gone when he returned.

Chapter 6
Wednesday Morning

Chris bolted out of bed with a song in his heart, pep in his step, and excitement in his loins. His face was gleaming with his infectious smile that had been a stranger for much too long. For the second time since he had been there, he was in love. This time he was sure that it was real. Ms. Walker was the one for him.

He was so happy that a song ricocheted from his heart to his lips, and he was singing loud enough to wake the dead. If not the dead, the sleeping Dora and Goldie, neither of whom was in the mood for an early morning concert. Goldie kicked Dora, and Dora in turn yelled at Chris, "If you don't stop that damned noise, I'm going to come in there and kick your little ass."

Love is wonderful. It fortifies the heart and the soul. The immediate effect it had on Chris was for the first time he ignored Dora. He decided to sing louder! Dora merely put her pillow over her head and went back to sleep. Goldie grunted, looked at her watch and got out of bed to get dressed.

Sonia slept well that night. Somehow she found peace, although her dreams confused her. She had dreamed that she was running around the track with Marcus. She seemed to have looked up in the clouds while running with Marcus. The clouds somehow had taken the form of Roy's face, and he seemed to be urging her on. He seemed to be saying, "Run on baby, run on! I'm fine, Sonia run!"

When her mother called her, she sat up in her bed with a quizzical smile on her face. "Marcus?" she smiled. Sonia could not believe that she had awakened with his name on her lips. " Well, he is kind of cute, " she laughed softly as she jumped out of bed. As she turned the water on for her shower, she thought about the time she had spent in that same shower with Roy. Her mood changed as she felt the hurt again. She could not enter it. Instead she ran down stairs where her mother was sitting at the table drinking coffee.

Like a cat, Sonia jumped on her mother's lap the way she did when she was much younger and much smaller. Virginia was caught completely by surprise and much of the coffee was now flowing across the table. She laughed, teasing Sonia by saying that she didn't know what she was going to do with her. The deejay on the radio announced that it was 6:10 and guaranteed that it was going to be a hot, hot day.

"Can we talk?" Sonia asked.

Virginia responded, "Sure, what do you want to talk about, baby?"

"You know about Roy, Little Al and everything. But you got to promise that you won't get mad!"

Virginia thought that she had been prepared for this conversation. She was told by Reverend and Mrs. Govens to expect Sonia to want to talk about the whole affair. They cautioned her that she needed a sympathetic ear at first. They advised her to just listen without passing judgment although what she would hear may shock, surprise, even anger her. Now, later, after the emotions had begun to subside, she should begin to adjust anything that the girl was doing that was wrong. However, the first thing she needed to do was to listen.

Sonia was amazingly candid, she told it all! She started from the time she hung around the basketball court where she had a female friend to introduce them. She told her mother that it was not hard ". . . to get him to think that I was seventeen or even older because I am so big. Also, I don't play with them children that is my age, and they know better than to say something."

Virginia was amazed at what Sonia was telling her, but she somehow managed to maintain her cool. Sonia told her about how the late Rommie used to ask her about going out with him. Still Virginia let her talk. Sonia told about the time that Roy came to their home, but only after he was convinced that she was Sonia's sister. Still Virginia maintained her cool. Sonia told her about the two of them showering together upstairs one night while she was working. At that point, Virginia lost it!

"Sonia, do you know that there are whores, prostitutes that don't have that kind of nerve! Don't you know that I work damned hard down at that bar; so that, you can have things and chances in life that I never had! You never seen me act like that around men, but I guess you see women like Dora acting like a dog in heat and treating people like shit and think that is the way. Sure, I don't have a lot of education but I got respect for myself. But there you are acting like a child that nobody loves or cares about. You think that Dora has got it made in the shade. Well, let me tell you . . . if you think that you are going to grow up to be nothing, you are mistaken. Damn it! From now on you are going to act, dress, go to school, and behave like a young lady or girl with good sense, or so help me I'll . . ."

With that Virginia told Sonia to go get ready for school. Sonia started slowly out of the room. Virginia jumped up from the chair that she was uneasily sitting in and grabbed her daughter.

She hugged Sonia with tears in her eyes and told her that she loved her very much and wanted the best for her. She apologized for not being there for her as much as she should have but promised that, too, would change.

Virginia was pleasantly surprised and gratified that Sonia cried and said to her, "I love you, too, mommy. I'll do better." The two hugged for a while longer. Sonia smiled at her mother as she skipped upstairs to prepare for school. This time taking her shower was no problem at all.

Marcus had fallen asleep with pictures of homes in his bed that his grandfather had collected. His grandfather had always dreamed that he would live in a nice place. A place where he would not have to hear the sounds of despair, hopelessness, and jeopardy seven days a week, twenty - four hours a day. He felt that a body needed quiet time for the soul to kind of get itself together in peace and quiet. Unfortunately, the only lasting peace and quiet many in the projects would know would be in the morgue, funeral home or the grave. He hated to complain, but he worked and still could not afford a nicer home for his grandson.

Often, he was close to giving up, only his faith kept him keeping on. His wife had died when his daughter was a young girl, after a long and costly illness. Somehow, he overcame that and single-handedly raised his daughter who grew up to be a loving, caring young woman. While attending a local college she met and fell in love with a young man from South Africa. He did not want his daughter to marry the man, but she did and soon they were the proud parents of Marcus.

Marcus brought the family together, and Jacque soon discovered that his son - in - law was a loving, caring, and intelligent man with whom he grew to love and respect. The two of them often talked about the various social ills of racism. The conversation that seemed to have a life of its own was the injustice and indignities of the South African system of apartheid. They would agree that it was demonic, and they agreed that it had to end.

One day his son - in - law announced that he was going home to do whatever he could to help end apartheid. He said that it hurt him to live in relative luxury while his family and friends were being denied even the most basic human rights. His plan was to go back, help cause the change, which he felt, would be soon, then come back to his wife and child. Jacque's daughter was furious, because she felt that her place was with her husband. She insisted that she and Marcus go with him.

Marcus was nearly five when they went to South Africa. Jacque was justifiable afraid for them. Every telephone call, every letter, and every silence had the potential of bearing ominous news. It came from the State Department. At first it was called ". . . an incident of suspicious nature."

A few days later, he received another call from a female from the State Department who regretted to inform him that his daughter and son - in - law were victims of ". . . a probable double homicide . . . an unfortunate tragedy." He was informed that unfortunately it would not be possible for the bodies to be shipped to the states. Also, they could not seem to locate his grandson. He never heard a word directly from the State Department again.

A few weeks later, he received a call from a church based group who asked him to meet them in Washington, D.C. as they had smuggled Marcus home. However, the immigration people needed proof that he was a citizen. They asked him if he had any documents that would prove he was the legal guardian of the boy. Fortunately, as a precaution, they had left all the requisite documentation with Jacque in case they had difficulty reentering the United States.

Jacque asked Michael to take him to get his grandson. The reunion was tearful but happy. His thick accent was a bit difficult for the men to understand at first. But as Marcus continued, he astonished both men with his obvious maturity and knowledge. Marcus told them about the horrible conditions in South Africa, but he spoke with optimism about the country's future. He related the horror of his parents being assassinated by the police. He talked about their political activities with pride often calling them martyrs.

The boy had from the time he arrived an unquenchable thirst for knowledge as he vowed to someday go back to South Africa and continue the struggle. He decided that he was going to be a doctor.

*

As if on cue, the three children met and started toward school. They did not talk too much as each was engrossed in their own thoughts. Chris could not wait to see Ms. Walker. Marcus was hoping that he would learn something at school this day. Sonia was completely confused as her heart had begun fluttering from the time she saw Marcus. She just did not know what she was going to do with herself.

Nadine's morning was filled with an eerie calm. The twins did not seem to have too much to say to each other. In fact, the three went about preparing themselves for the day like strangers in an old-fashioned boarder home. Several times she wanted to call Tracey, but she just could not do it. Shala announced rather dryly that she would be catching the bus. Nadine gave them both money and walked out the door to her car in silence.

On her way to work she wondered aloud what else could go wrong. She honestly considered asking her ex to take custody of the twins. After all, she had them since the breakup; he and ` Miss Thing 'could better afford them than she. She had decided to make the call as she pulled into the school parking lot.

As she walked toward the building, a very gruff voice called out to her, "Hey, teach, we need to talk!" Goldie was stepping out of her automobile with her now homicidal looking right-hand man, the infamous Snake. Goldie dressed in a dark blue sweat suit walked slowly towards the now frightened Nadine saying, "Well, teach we got us some business to talk about."

"I know, but you don't worry. I will pay your money back as soon."

"Look teach, I know you ain't got shit, so let's cut the crap." By now, Goldie was standing as close as she could to Nadine without touching her.

As Goldie spoke, Snake circled Nadine and was between her and the door while admiring her.

"Look a little nervous teach, don't get your fine, pretty self upset. Ain't nobody gonna bother you. Unless you get . . ."

"I'll have your money when I get . . ."

"Is that anyway to talk to a new friend, Miss Sweet Teach. I ain't hardly worried about that chump change that I laid on you. If I was worried, Snake here would, uh, take care of it for me. That's what I pay him for and he good, real good. Ask anybody, he good."

(Snake grunted for effect.)

"I'll get at you later to let you know how we gonna settle this little thing," Goldie said smiling as she tried to sneak in a little kiss on the cheek. Nadine turned her head in disgust.

"Don't worry, baby, they all start with me like that, but we is gonna be good friends 'fore it all over, Teach," Goldie declared as she started walking away from her.

Snake lustfully, checked Nadine out again, smiled and sort of whispered to her, "Bet you all freak, teach."

Nadine was overwhelmed with fear as she watch the luxury automobile containing her tormentors glide away. Nadine composed herself as she walked into the building. Standing in the hallway in front of the office was the principal and Mr. Maos. Before she could speak, Mr. Franks handed her an envelope and informed her that she was to report to a Mr. Jones at school headquarters. As he turned to walk away from her, almost seemingly an afterthought, he informed her that she was being relieved of all of her teaching duties. Stunned she heard but did not comprehend Mr. Maos was saying about a complaint number.

Early that morning Tracey's eyes opened easily and carefree, as she were one satisfied woman. She was well blessed married to and loved by a man like Johnny. She eased away from his embrace, as he really deserved it after the way he had made her feel. She always likes to watch him sleep. He looked just like an innocent child. It was times like this that it was hard to imagine that he was a cop, a very tough cop, working in one of the most crime infested areas of the city, but that's what he wanted to do. It was his ways of giving something back, his contribution to the city that he loved. Finally, she had to wake him as he was going to take her to work.

She kissed and hugged her man, "You better get yourself out of this bed before I . . ."

"Before you what? " he answered as he rolled on top of her. She giggled, "Before I put you on house arrest!"

Again they made LOVE as if there was not going to be a tomorrow.

Johnny teased her about singing in the plain patrol car as they were on their way to school. As she was getting that last a.m. kiss in front of the school, she noticed a tearful Nadine slowly walking toward them.

Nadine looked bewildered. As she got closer to Tracey, she moaned, "I guess I have really done it this time. I am gone."

Tracey watched her run toward her car. She looked back at Johnny who nodded knowingly.

Tracey dropped her belongings and ran after Nadine. She caught her as she was fumbling through her purse for her keys.

She grabbed the taller Nadine and spinning her around. "Look, You may have messed up, really messed up but you need to do what you have to do to straighten this thing up . . ."

"Mr. Franks just told me that I don't have a job! What the hell is I'm going to do?"

"Look, he cannot fire you, he did not hire you. But you need to get yourself straight spiritually. Pray to God for forgiveness. We will be praying for you, too! Things will work out! I promise you, Nadine, things will indeed work out!"

With the innocence of a child Nadine appealed, "You really think so. I was . . ."

"Don't matter, He will take care of you, because He loves you, Nadine! And I love you, too!"

Johnny had picked up his wife's belongings and was standing beside them. "Nadine, you are about the most difficult people in the world to understand sometimes, but we both love you. Anything we can do to help, we will. But remember the He is in charge, and He is able."

With that he put his massive arms around both.

Nadine wiped the tears from her eyes and thanked them for their love and concern.

They watched her as she drove away. Nadine surprised herself as she began to hum a hymn that she did not even remember that she remembered, "All Is Well With My Soul."

She felt stronger, much stronger.

Chapter 7
Been Dead

At about eleven in the morning, Michael was on his way to pick up Jacque. He loved Jacque as he had always been that friend, the one who had his back when needed, who listened when necessary, who cried with him, who laughed with him, and enjoyed his victories without envy or jealousy. He paused as he passed the corner on which his son had been murdered. The red stains of Roy's blood could still be seen on the sidewalk.

Michael wiped the tears from his eyes. The lost of his son was very hard on him. He had to keep on reminding himself that God was in charge and He is certainly able. A little boy aimlessly walking down the street distracted him. The little boy was obviously not going to school, as it was very late. His heart went out to the child as he looked very unkept and dirty. He stepped out of the car to speak to the boy, but upon seeing him the boy ran. He shook his head sadly, got back into his car, and continued his drive to meet with Jacque.

The drive through the old neighborhood was full of ghosts both of cheer and melancholy. He wished that things were now as they had been when he was a child. He laughed to himself as he recalled that the most notorious man then was the number's man. The number's man had an air of gangsterism but never bothered anybody, save those poor souls who did not pay up. He recalled during that time, the worse thing that usually happened to a body was a good old-fashioned butt - kicking. Sometimes it was a group effort. But still, all one would get was his butt kicked. He sadly said to himself, "Well   that was then and this, God save us, is now."

As Michael got out of his car and walked toward Jacque's home, he looked around at the neglect, the filth, and the debris. He wondered aloud "Why?" There were some folk aimlessly standing, milling around. A few spoke to him, saying that they would be in church ". . . as soon as they got it together." He responded by telling them that they were always welcomed in God's house and invited them to come pass; even if, they just wanted to talk.

A stranger walked over to Michael and offered him his condolences. The man nervously looked around to be sure that no one saw him talking to Michael. He said that they needed to talk in private, ". . . not here, not now but we need to talk." Michael noticed that the man was a little to well dressed to belong there. He looked around cautiously and almost ran away.

There were many things going through Michael's mind as he knocked on the door. Jacque opened the door with his customary grin and the two hugged, and exchanged greetings.

"Ready?" Michael asked.

"Well, as ready as I'm going to be. Let's go." Jacque responded.

"Have you had any thoughts about where you want to live?"

Jacque laughed and spread his arms, "And leave all this? Are you crazy? I'm going to stay here!" Michael looked at his friend and laughed.

"Don't look at me like I'm a crazy person. Sure, we are going to leave, but right now, I don't have a clue as to where. I want to be far enough away not to be in the middle of this battle zone out here, but close enough that the boy and me don't lose contact. You know what I mean? Do you know somebody that I can see about a house?"

"Jacque, you know that my wife's cousin is the best. Just call him." After saying that, Michael shut down. Jacque continued to talk but there was no response from Michael as he began to drive.

"Brakes, Mike! Stop, damned the car!" Jacque screamed at Michael who had gone through a red light.

"Uh, what?" Michael reacted as if being revived from a deep sleep. Suddenly, realizing the predicament that they were in, he slammed on the brakes. He looked at his friend apologetically and suggested that he drive instead. Jacque smiled as he got out of the car, and the two hugged as they passed each other.

"You are right, you know," Michael said dryly as they continued.

"Keep in mind, Reverend Doctor, you like all of us on this life's trip are only a man. Just a man, and ain't perfect. So, stop being so hard on yourself."

"You do not understand, or maybe you do. I don't know, but I don't know what I'm going to say tonight."

"You mean at the funeral?"

"I have been telling grieving folk that they needed to put God first even as things look very dark. I tell them to" . . . put their hearts in His hands. I say, "Be ye of good faith in the Lord and He will see you through."

"I'm not sure what you are getting to. I mean, you believe what you said to those folks didn't you?"

"Well, if my advice is good for others, shouldn't it be good for me? I mean I tell folks to be joyous in their suffering, because God will see you through. Joy; am I crazy, or even worse a hypocrite? I am so upset, so confused that I wish I could go somewhere and just hide!"

"Michael," Jacque responded gently, "we all fantasize about running away from trouble, but we can never run away from our selves."

Michael began to cry softly while reaching into his glove compartment for a tissue. Jacque continued, "Will you answer one question for me?"

Michael nodded.

"Well, I have heard you talk about faith, joy in your sermons and joy sometimes when you are talking to folks who are troubled, you see. Now, I'm sure that I understand this faith thing. Maybe the only reason that I'm alive and sane is my faith. But about this joy thing? Exactly what is joy? Does joy always mean that you are happy all the time, because you have a personal relationship with God Almighty and nothing can cause you pain? Tell me, my brother, what does it mean?"

Michael thought for a moment, and then he began to speak in a monotone voice that lacked conviction, "When speaking of joy that way, one is not talking about the kind of joy that makes you want to laugh, giggle, or joke around . . . It's about." Suddenly he stopped talking and gazed out of the window. He thought that he saw the same little boy whom he had seen earlier, but he dismissed the thought.

He turned his entire body toward Jacque. Jacque could feel a surge of energy, optimism emulating from him. With a staccato voice, Michael began, "We are taught that this kind of joy means confidence in our God. Knowing He is with us through thick and thin. (Now with a smile) Like I used to tell Roy. It may look very dark, and there seems to be no way out. But! Using a sport's analogy, if you know that you know that your team is going to win in the end, what difference does the score make?

"Looks like Satan has got all the bases covered and we, sometimes we feel like we are flying though the hot coals of hell itself wearing gasoline underwear! We feel hopeless and helpless and just about time we are ready . . . 'we be ready to get all crispy burnt, He steps in and with one mighty breath, cools those flames and fires of destruction! And He makes a way out of no way!"

Michael clapped his hands with jubilation!

Jacque laughed aloud, "Now, there you go, my man!"

Arriving at their destination, Jacque maneuvered the car gently through the circular driveway and stopped in front of the very large, traditional, old money, and well-appointed rancher. Trees, snuggled by all types of beautiful flowers and greenery, surrounded it.

"Now, here is a home!" Jacque exclaimed.

"Beautiful, isn't it?" Michael responded.

Michael straightened his tie as they walked toward the door. Jacque almost tripped over himself a couple of times as he was admiring the home and the grounds. "Is there a swimming pool around here somewhere?" Jacque wondered aloud.

As if to answer his question, from around the west side of the house appeared a tall (Jacque guessed that she was somewhere between 5'7-9"), very silky dark, very attractive, middle-aged woman wearing a wet yellow bikini with a matching towel casually draped around her shoulders. Her appearance caused Jacque to choke, which embarrassed him.

With a broad smile, which showed off her pearly white teeth, she looked at Michael first while offering him her hand, "Why Reverend Govans. It has been much too long. I very much enjoyed our last meeting, our little talk." Then turning to Jacque, "You must be Jacque. I have heard a lot about you. As you see, I was taking a little dip. I am very sorry that I am not more presentable. Will you please forgive me?"

"Why certainly, Mrs. Johnson. It really did not seem to be as warm until I saw you," Michael offered. Jacque shook his head in agreement.

"You are such a flatterer. But please call me Violet. There have been scores of, well; you cannot imagine how many police types that have been here calling on me, Mrs. Jerome David Johnson. Man! I should advise you that your pictures are being taken by those nice officers over there."

Both followed her extended arm with their eyes. Sure enough there was a sedan with a guy taking pictures.

"Let's go around back where we can have a little privacy."

After they finished the small talk, Michael asked her if she had reconsidered claiming the remains of Rommie. Still smiling, she complimented him for being such a good friend to her late husband, she told me that she would donate money to his church for troubled youth in his name ". . . to give a little something back, but under no circumstances would she have anything to do with his body."

Neither man could hide the disappointment they were feeling.

"Now, gentlemen, the last time I saw my infamous late husband was about four nearly five years ago. He came running in here with half of the police department chasing him. He jumped under the bed like a child, a scared little child. (She laughed.) The police almost shot me! Now, when all the confusion was over, and it, I should say out of respect, Rommie was safely under my bed, (She laughed again, but louder.) He had the nerve to start talking smack to them!

"The police snatched that butt, kicked it while I just laid in my bed laughing. If he was going to be bad, he should have done it somewhere other than in my bedroom!"

She stopped for a moment to compose herself, "Now, my father worked very, very hard for all this. Sometimes, we did not see him for days, and his businesses were right here. He had plans, big plans for me. He sent me to the better schools and use to challenge me, saying that I was going to be somebody, somebody really and truly important. He wanted me to be a credit to my race."

Although her demeanor was now pleasant, but there was a definite aura of anguish and defiance in her voice. Both wanted to but dared not stop her. Jacque could only watch this amazing woman, everything about her was just right and wonderful, and she certainly noticed him checking her out.

"Like many kids who have all of the advantages, I went to the best private school and was often the only Black student which was fine with me. Fine with me because all of those white folks wanted to do me, because I have always been fine. I would go to their homes and bring white kids home all the time. My daddy had visions of me marrying a white successful doctor, lawyer, or maybe businessman, which again was fine with me. Since we were so, uh, a need a word, progressive, yes, my first intimate experiences were right upstairs in my room. There was very little intercourse, but we . . ."

She stopped, reached over and touched Jacque on his upper thigh, which absolutely ignited a fire.

"Please forgive me. I must be embarrassing you. Sometimes I just go on and." Michael accepted her apology as she laughed, saying that she was talking to Jacque.

"Anyway, I met Rommie at a party which would have made my father have a major heart attack! We spent a little private time together, and like they say, once you go Black, you can never . . ."

They all laughed.

"When I brought my shiny Black knight home, my father looked at him oddly and left the room without saying a word. My mother looked at us both and left the room, also.

"I was forbidden to even mention his name around them. Anyway, I was so angry that I married him the very next day. The man did not have a place to lay his head. Said after we eloped that he always stayed with his woman. So I came home where he surely could not.

"He was shocked when he found out I was having Naomi, who is not his child. I never told anybody who the father was, but I think Rommie found out. Her father was one of the world's finest Black entertainers. Queer as a three-dollar bill. It took quite a bit of, um, doing to get him to . . . anyway."

"But that day four nearly five years ago, when the police dragged his ass out of here, he died as far as I am concerned. He called a few times. The last time a couple of weeks ago, telling me that he was sorry about everything that he had done, but you can never take the word of a thug. I hung up while he was talking about getting out of the business. I really have no interest in that body down there in the morgue. My husband is dead, but he has been dead as far as I'm concerned.

"If it means that I will go to hell for not attending to him, too bad! Like I said my husband has been dead!"

Michael asked if he could make the arrangements. "I'll take care of it all, and you will not . . ."

She looked at him carefully. "Will you gentlemen excuse me for a moment?" She said as she walked toward the house. She looked back with a half smile.

While waiting, Jacque asked Michael if he thought she had changed her mind. Michael just shook his head. After about ten minutes Violet returned with a pitcher of lemonade and glasses. Smiling, she poured both a drink. Violet sat with them sipping her drink, smiling like the cat, which had swallowed the canary, which made Michael a bit uneasy.

"What's going on?" He finally asked as Jacque looked at her with that look.

Suddenly, she began to giggle, then laughed aloud. "Excuse me, and maybe God will forgive me for being too vengeful, but I have made what I believe are appropriate arrangements for that bas . . . my husband."

Violet waited like a cobra for the proper moment to strike. She waited patiently for one of her guests to ask about the appropriate arrangements. Finally, Jacque did.

With a most gracious smile, "I called my lawyer. He is going to arrange to have Jerome cremated. The undertaker is instructed to put the ashes in a greasy bag and dump them in the dumpster down there in the projects where his beloved Dora lives."

Michael started to speak, but she gently placed her finger over his mouth. "And when they find his car, I will have it delivered to you to dispose with as you please. I will send money and if you do not need the car, junk it, sell it, or give it away."

"Now, if you gentlemen will excuse me, I have a thousand things to do. Please see your way out."

Michael opened his mouth to protest again. She stopped him again, "Like I said, he has been dead to me. Please leave little old widow me alone to celebrate like a heathen!"

Flirting with Jacque with a most sensuous smile, "Jacque, you must come pass. I'm sure that we can find a little something to (winking) do."

"Maybe I will," he responded.

"Please come pass the church sometimes," Michael offered.

"Little old widow me?" she responded gazing into Jacques's eyes, "you'll got good fire insurance?" she walked away laughing.

Michael knowingly smiled as Jacque watched her carefully as she walked away like a goddess, a beautiful Black goddess. As they rode toward the inner world, Jacque looked at Michael wondering aloud if he should take the lady up on her offer. Michael laughed.

"It's not like I'm seeing her behind Rommie's back. She is really so fine!"

"I am not your conscious, my man. And, you certainly do not need my permission to do whatever you please."

Jacques laughed, "Good thing you be a preacher man, you had to be 'cause you sure a party pooper!"

As they headed toward the projects they recalled and laughed about many things they had done as teenagers. His seeing the same little boy he was constantly encountering interrupted Michael's laughter. "You know that kid?" He quickly asked Jacques. Jacques looked around but could not see the child, "exactly what kid are you talking about?"

"He was just over . . . oh, never mind!"

Chapter 8
Playing . . .

Michael heard a young boy's voice calling to him, "Mister Hey mister!" He stopped dead in his tracks on the steps of his church. He looked around and saw the same seemingly unkept little boy that he kept seeing off and on that afternoon sitting on the very bottom step to his left. The boy's head was between his legs with his arms wrapped around them as if he were cold although it was ninety degrees. Michael walked toward the boy while smiling.

The boy turned his head toward Michael and with almost no expression, "Mister, is you something in that church?"

Michael laughed gently, "Yes, I am something in that church. I am the pastor."

Looking up at him, the little boy pondered the response, and then asked, "That's the same as the preacher, ain't it? I seen you, I think, on some Sundays out here wearing robes and stuff something like them wrestlers wear on TV."

"Yes, and what's your name, sir?"

"I'm Denny and you know good and well that I ain't no sir. I'm just a little boy."

Michael sat on a step near the boy, but as he sat, the boy moved a bit further away.

Michael noticed and asked the boy if he minded him sitting near him. The boy shrugged his shoulders and answered that he could sit where he wanted if he was really the preacher of this church.

"Anyway," the boy began, "this morning. last night I could not sleep and when my mother came home this morning I told her and she was mad or something and started screaming at me. She tried to smack me but I'm too fast for her. Then she tried to hit me with her shoe that she throwed at me, but I'm too fast for that too! She hasn't been able to hit me with nothing since I was a little boy (he said with pride)! Not less she sneaks me while I'm sleep or sick or something!

"Well, I was gonna to tell her anyhow. She was too tired to keep throwing shit at me. So, when she was in the chair I kept telling her I was up 'cause I kept having these bad dreams."

"Do you want to talk about it?" Michael asked.

Looking at Michael like he was really stupid, the boy responded, "That's why I'm here, my mama told me to go tell a preacher about my problems and leave her the hell alone!"

Michael cleared his voice, "All right let's talk. You want to go inside?"

"No, I ain't going in there . . . I ain't got no church clothes or nothing. What would I do in there?"

"So, what would you like to talk about?"

"You know that man that got hisself kilt down around the corner?"

Michael nodded.

"I was there when it happened. I told 5 - 0 about it when they took me down to the station. They gave me some hamburgers while I was talking to them."

Michael stood up. "Don't move Denny. I'm going to ring the bell and get the secretary to get some hamburgers for us."

As he quickly walked up the stairs the boy asked him if they could get some fries and a soda. Michael answered, "Anything, anything at all!"

He returned as quickly as he could, but this time he sat closer to the boy. As if reviewing a thrilling television show or a movie, the boy was very animated in describing in detail his account of the murder of the man! Denny had no idea that the man the he was describing was Michael 's son, The boy was so involved in his account that he showed the actions of Roy and Little Al.

It was like something was tearing Michael's heart out as the boy played out the murder. Michael flinched as Denny stood over the "Man" firing the lethal shots into his body. He then stretched out on the ground as if he were the victim. Finally, Denny showed how the drugs and money were planted on the body.

Although in his heart and soul Michael knew that his son had not been involved in the nefarious drug business, he was relieved to hear from the mouth of this child the actual account of what really happened. He silently thanked God for this revelation.

When Ms. Thorn, the church secretary, opened the door and looked down, she saw a little boy waving his arms and pretending to shoot an imaginary pistol into the ground while Michael sat on the steps watching. She could only see the back of his head, and then the boy stretch out on the ground. Concerned, she ran down the steps, "What in the world are you two doing?"

"It's, uh, it's fine Ms. Thorne, my friend was showing . . ."

Denny interrupted smiling, "That your girlfriend? She sure a real fine bitch! I wouldn't mind hav . . ."

"Denny!" Michael interrupted, "this is Ms. Thorne, the church secretary. We should not call women that. It does not show respect and most do not like it. Would you like to apologize to the lady?"

Denny looked at him quizzically, then at her pondering what he should do. "Well," he began looking her in the eyes and smiling, "I'm sorry but you is one fine bi. Lady! What is a church secretary? Is that like a girlfriend?"

Ms. Thorne bent over and kissed Denny on what appeared to be a clean spot on his forehead, "Thanks for the compliment, but like the reverend said, we don't like to be called that "b" word. And I think you are a cutesy pie yourself.'

Denny beamed.

Reaching into his pocket, Michael laughed, "Before you two get engaged and married, Ms. Thorne, will you run down to the nearest fast food place and get us some hamburgers, fries, and sodas."

Looking down at Denny, "And get yourself something, on my friend, with your fine self. (They all laughed!) Use my car, I just got out of it, and it should not be too hot!"

Michael looked at the boy smiling at him as he reminded him of Rommie when he was about his age.

Denny frowned at him and yelled, "Why you smiling at me? You funny or something?"

"What?"

"Is you funny or something?" the boy repeated defiantly.

"No, why did you?"

"Well, how come you was smiling at me?"

"Because, young man, you remind me of somebody?"

"You got a little boy?"

Ms. Thorne seeing, the pain in Michael face volunteered to take the boy with her.

As they drove away, Michael mumbled, "Yes, I have a boy, but he is with God now."

Meanwhile, Dora was at home alone drinking the last of the booze and smoking her last cigarette. She danced around the living room to one of her favorite oldies. While dancing around the room, she noticed that Rommie's car keys were still there. She picked them up and tossed them into the air while remembering that Rommie usually kept a carton of cigarettes, and sometimes other little "treats" in his trunk.

"He sure don't need no smokes or nothing else where he's at down there," she laughed.

She continued to laugh as she strolled out to the car. She paused as she approached the car remembering some of the fun things they used to do in it. She opened the driver's door and sat down remembering the first time Rommie let her drive it. She turned on the ignition switch and the motor purred. She noticed that it was full of gas as Rommie always kept it full "just in case."

She got out, locked the door, and she walked towards the trunk. She opened the trunk, and sure enough, lying there was a couple of cartoons of cigarettes. She also noticed a couple bottles of champagne, a fifth of brandy, and a blanket covering what looked a box. Her heart began to race as she lifted the blanket. There staring her in the face was his attaché' case. She looked suspiciously and cautiously around as she lifted it out of the trunk. She closed it with her arms full of the bounty from the car.

Her heart raced and water flowed from her forehead to her toes as she anticipated having the mother load of drugs right there in her hand. All she had to do was to off it and BOY! One thing she knew for sure that she was not giving Goldie SHIT!

She closed and locked the door. Once inside, she ran into her room and slammed that door shut! She throw the case on her bed and.... the telephone rang! She looked at it, laughed, and screamed at it, "Goldie, we ain't doing shit tonight or any other night with your monkey looking ass!"

She tried to open the case, but the damned case was locked!

"Keys! Keys!" She yelled as she remembered that she had left them in the trunk in her haste to get away. "Calm down," she said to herself while trying to decided whether to take the case with her to the car. She felt that she would have to hurry as one of them thieving bastards might steal the car.

She threw the case into her closet and bolted through her living room and out the door. Arriving at the car, she was relieved to see that the keys were still there. She snatched them and ran towards her home. A couple of guys who happened by were amused and entertained by seeing her running. "Must be jelly 'cause jam don't shake like that. Needless to say, Dora was not amused.

Out of breath, exhausted with shot nerves, she finally found the key to open the case. Just as she was about to open it, she heard the door open. She almost had a heart attack!

"Who in the hell is it?" she yelled.

"Me, Dora," Chris answered.

She jumped up ran to her door, opened it carefully, and eyed Chris suspiciously. "What the hell you doing here?"

He saw that she was so wet that her clothes were sticking to her. Her hair which was usually neat and straight was now wild looking and curly. She was breathing heavily, and she was redder than he had ever seen her. She was madder than a wet hen! And with the wild look in her eyes, he quickly decided that he needed to be someplace else! He threw his stuff in his hands on the couch and retreated towards the door. She raced towards the door, slammed it shut and locked it!

From a safe distance, Chris looked back at the door deciding that Dora had finally completely lost her mind! He walked slowly towards Marcus house not even noticing the approaching Sonia. Safely in her room, Dora opened the case. The contents almost caused her a major heart attack! Inside the case was MONEY! Rolls and stacks of MONEY! FIFTIES! HUNDREDS! More money than she had ever imagined existed! The case was jammed and packed with MONEY!

"Damned you Rommie! Wherever, you be down there in hell, I'll be there with you, but before I get there, I'm gonna live a rich bitch!" She threw some of it up in the air while laughing and now singing and dancing around the room!

"First thing I'm going to do is to get my ass out of these damned projects!" she purred to her image in the mirror. "Then, I'm going to.... SHIT! Chris! What in the hell am I going to do with his little ass!"

She popped the cork on one of the bottles of champagne. As The foam sizzled and splashed all over her, she began to ponder where she was going to plant Chris as she began her life as a rich bitch! She opened the bottle of brandy and guzzled down a swallow or two!

"I have gone from a poor.... from zero to real rich bitch in seven seconds flat! Finally, I am what a was born to be, suppose to be, a rich bitch!"

She noticed a sheet of paper in the case. It was a total sheet that damned near made her faint!

She sipped some of the hot champagne while she paced the floor thinking. "First I gotta do is to get out of Dodge," she said. "But first, what in the hell do I do with Chris? Shit!"

Just about then there was a knock on the door. She stood there for a while wondering what to do. Again, she heard the light tapping on her door. "What to do?" she thought. She knew that it was not Goldie as Goldie would be trying to tear the damned door down by now, thinking that she had some man in there. "Must be the worrisome Chris," she thought.

She covered the case with her blanket, closed her bedroom door and walked towards the door. She could see that it was a man. Damned! Near panicked, she slid along the wall to get a better look. Soon, she recognized Jacque.

"WHAT THE FU...! Wait!"

She eased the door open, looked around and snatched an astonished Jacque in the door, slamming it behind him. At that point and time, Jacque had to agree with Chris' opinion that Dora had lost or was losing her mind!

After the initial shock of being snatched into Dora's home, a place that he had never been, he turned his head away from her as she wearing only her shorts. Undaunted, she grabbed his hand and led him to the couch while apologizing for all the bad blood they had between them. She took all the blame for everything, including the times that she had called him a bunch of names and the time that she had thrown a bottle at him for no apparent reason.

While he sat there apprehensively trying to figure out what was going on, Dora turned on all the charm she could muster. "Uh, Jacque, I think that the reason that I have been such a bitch to you is that you, uh, scared me. I mean, you are about the strongest man that I have ever known. I just did not know how to take you. Do you know what I'm saying?"

A completely perplexed Jacque began, "Dora, I just came over here to..."

Suddenly, Dora jumped up, asked him to excuse her for a minute and ran into her room. While she was in motion, Jacque thought to himself that she was, indeed a very gorgeous woman. He was surprised to see that she was as firm as she was given the obvious abuse that she had put her body though.

"Fine, so fine," he thought, "but the pure devil. Wonders what she wants?"

She came out of her room with a cigarette in her mouth and a bottle of brandy in her hands with a smile that was almost angelic.

"One more little moment," she smiled as she went into the kitchen, returning with two glasses.

"Want a drink?" she smiled as she sat beside the now extremely apprehensive Jacque. He stood and began again, "Dora, Chris came over to my place upset. He felt something was a little off here."

He paused as he totally expected her to take off on him, but she was amazingly cool for a woman who did not like him, who was half nude, and obviously drunk, high, or extremely horny. "So, I came over to see what was going on and maybe..."

"Jacque, I'm okay, really, want a drink?"

Jacque accepted and totaled the drink, which surprised him.

While trying to figure out her next move, she poured herself a drink and stood up. She glanced into the mirror and saw that she was topless. Damned, no wonder!

"Jacque" she said as she made an unconvincing attempt to cover herself while scurrying towards her door, "you must think that I'm a very bad woman."

Reentering the room with a translucent robe, "Really, things have been so...so... upset I did not know that I was..." she lowered her head to appear to be embarrassed. "I'm so embarrassed."

"Think nothing of it. I know that we can somehow get distracted. But like I was saying, Chris asked me to come over to see if you were okay. I can see that something is bothering you, would you like to talk about it?"

Jacque walked home knowing that he had done a good thing. He had agreed to keep Chris for a few days while she went to Georgia to see about her very, ill father. As he entered the door, he told Chris to go get some of his clothes and his schoolbooks, as he would be staying with them for a while.

It never occurred to Chris to ask why, and Dora told Jacque not to tell him for fear that he would be too upset. She told him that she would call in a few days to tell him what was happening. Chris took Marcus with him to retrieve his belongings. Chris wished that this arrangement would be permanent; at least, until Christee could come to get him.

By the time Chris and Marcus had gathered his belongings, Dora had showered and dressed. She was wearing the white outfit that she had worn to her mother's funeral. Marcus was impressed by how beautiful she looked and told her so. She thanked and hugged him and kissed and hugged Chris. It felt good to him; even though, it was the first time she had shown him any affection.

She put an envelope in his bag and asked him to give it to Jacque in the morning. She hugged him again, picked up the attaché' case and walked to the door behind them. She closed the door, then reopened it and threw the keys inside.

Later as the three were eating, Chris remembered the envelope that Dora had given him to give to Jacque. Jacque opened it and saw that there was quite a bit of money in it. The boys had not noticed.

He asked Chris about his grandfather, and Chris told him that he had been killed a while ago in a car wreck.

Jacque excused himself from the table, reminded the boys to get dressed for the funeral, and quickly walked upstairs to his room. He sat in the chair next to the window, and began to cry, "Like I said, Dora is the pure evil."

Nadine about this time was sitting in her kitchen, drinking a cup of coffee and reflecting upon her day. After she had arrived at the school headquarters, she stood nervously outside. Convinced that she would be fired, her concern was what she was going to do next. With no job, she was sure that she would lose her heavily mortgaged home, her daughters would have to go live with their father, and she would be in the streets.

As she waited in the outer office to be interviewed, a woman exited the office that she was about to go in sobbing. The woman who looked familiar turned her head away from Nadine as she left the office. The receptionist picked up a folder and asked Nadine to follow her into the office.

The man behind the desk peered over his glasses at her as he invited her to sit down while adjusting his tie. Smiling, he asked her if she wanted a cup of coffee or something. She declined, but he insisted as he straightened his hair with his hand. He stood and tripped over a plant that was beside his desk. He mumbled something about being clumsy as he walked to the door to ask the receptionist to brew a pot of coffee.

"Ms. Walker," he began obviously jittery, "we, that is, you, uh, know the reason for us having this little informal talk. We must be sure that our children have the best possible...What is that you are wearing?"

Puzzled, Nadine asked him what he meant.

"The fragrance you are wearing, I find you, I mean it, a refreshing change from, uh, what I...You know what I mean?"

Nadine smiled at him, knowing full well that the last thing that this lusty soul was going to do was to place her job in jeopardy. With her most charismatic smile, she told him that it was just a little something that one of her daughters had given her for her birthday. He inquired about the ages of her children and she told him a bit about her teenaged, twin girls.

Probing nervously, he remarked that she and her husband must have their hands full with the girls. He added that she did not seem to be old enough to have teenaged girls. She thanked him for the compliment, then informed him the she was divorced. She could see the relief on his face. So, she added that he had remarried. The guy looked just like he had just received some cash money.

"There are some things that you can tell about a person," he began, "just by talking to her. Now, with this uh, little incident, I don't see you as a scoundrel. Therefore, I am going to recommend that, see to it that this little matter is dropped. Further, How long have you been teaching?"

"For about fifteen years."

"Really? Do you think that this little incident will cause you any, uh, discomfort back there at your school?"

"I don't think so."

"Well, if you find that it does give me a little call and I will find you another assignment, some of these are out of the classroom and pay more So, even if things go well, but you feel that you need a change please let me know."

"Thank you."

"Now, did you drive here?"

She nodded.

"Well, I do not believe that you should go back to work today. Listen, I have another interview to take care of. It will not take me long. There's a little restaurant around the corner from here that I'm sure that you would love. Why don't I take care of my next appointment, write up my recommendation, and meet you?"

She waited for him to insist a couple of times before she agreed. He picked up the telephone, made the reservation, told her what to do when she arrived, and tripped over that same plant as he escorted her to the door. The receptionist rolled her eyes at them as she was bringing them coffee.

He brought a couple of his male co-worker with him.

She ignored much of their conversation, as it was all about her beauty, charm, and how lucky a man would be with her on his arm. Her host could not have been prouder if he had single - handedly figured out a way to solve world poverty or war. They all agreed the she was an asset to the school system. But she enjoyed a fabulous lunch. They all agreed that she was in line for a promotion. Man!

Well, that aside, she re-reads the copy of the letter that was being sent to her principal. One would have never guessed that her very job had been in jeopardy by the tone and content of the letter.

One would have guessed that she had passed a job interview. However, through all of this, she could not stop thinking about Chris. She could just get in her car, go find him, and hug his neck with his young, cute self. The idea of her finding the boy attractive frightened her, but what could she do? She shook her head as she found herself calculating the length of time it would take for him to be eighteen. Now, with all things going on in her life, she sure did not need this. But, again, what was she going to do?

Chapter 9
Stiffing and Jiving

As they arrived at the church in the limousine too late for the wake, Michael and Juanita, felt grateful and Blessed, as the whole area surrounding the church was full of parked vehicles of folk. He knew that many were mourners, well-wishers, the curious, and cynics. In addition to that he noticed limousines and official vehicles belonging to local and state officials as well as the news media. She was appreciative that so many had come to say good-bye to her boy.

As they were escorted into the packed and jammed church, Juanita froze as she saw the lonely closed casket surrounded by scores and scores of floral arrangements. The combined fragrances of them combined with the perfumes, colognes, and smells of the crowded edifice almost caused her to gag. The air conditioning did its best to cool the church, but it was too hot, too humid, and too crowded.

Save the mournful cries of the organ, the church became almost completely silent as the multitude recognized the couple. As they made their way to the front, many hugged, kissed, shook their hands, and offered their condolences. Michael was concerned for his wife as she was struggling to maintain her composure. Prior to leaving their home, she had been in an emotional quandary. She was so upset that at one point she had decided that she would not attend the funeral. It took a lot of prayer, conversation, and patience for her to get there. Now, he was not at all certain of how well or for how long she would hold out.

Sitting in the pulpit, he gazed out at the congregation as the seemingly endless acknowledgments and speeches were presented. Afterwards, a young lady, a close friend of Roy's sang a stirring rendition of "How Great Thou Art".

Michael began to feel a surge of POWER! As a prayer was being offered, he felt a sensation of restlessness flow through his body. He looked at the smiling face of his son on the front of the obituary, and he became totally oblivious to everything else that was going on.

The bishop, who was sitting next to him gently touched him on the arm, "Michael are you ready? Do you want to do this? If you don't feel up to it, I'll do it?"

Now standing in front of the congregation Michael began slowly, "My wife and I thank you very much for your outpouring of Love during what has been a very difficult time for us. We may never be able to thank each of you personally. Please do not hold it against us if we do not get to you.... uh... personally. May God bless you all for being so generous and caring.

The church was completely silent as Michael paused, turned his back to them and looked, admired the stained glass representation of Jesus Christ.

"This experience has reminded me that we are in spiritual warfare. This experience has reminded me that in this spiritual war our biggest, greatest enemies are the nefarious twins fear and doubt. Yes, fear and doubt. I have spent much time deciding and planning what I was going to do and say here this evening. I have a well-prepared sermon that's going, well, that I will not be using. I believe that the Holy Spirit has guided me in another direction.

"When I was a teenager, there was a popular expression that was used by, I guess, mostly Black folk, 'Stiffing and jiving'.

Stiffing and jiving meant that a body was not doing much but maybe talking loud and saying, doing nothing. We would often just lie around talking about what we would do 'if' and that was it not action accompanied our talk. Or we would play like we were doing something when all along we were Stiffing and jiving.

"Every Sunday the choirs sing their hearts out while the ushers are ushering their hearts out, the deacons are deaconing, and we up here sometimes get the Word right. Right here in the middle of crime, social and moral decay, we are in here isolated from the world just Stiffing and jiving. We drive right pass the homeless, the disadvantaged, the hopeless, and all the urban blight which is the visible evidence of the fact that we are engaged in a spiritual war.

"OH! But we understand that as long as we, God's army, remain in constant...pre - training, just talking about but not doing too much, we are just Stiffing and jiving! We, we say in this place that ". He is able." and that he will protect us..." if God be for us, who can be against us? ... But we are scared to death to even make our front steps safe for our children and us. ' Cause we are Stiffing and jiving.

"The mighty, mighty church stands in constant pre - readiness, we stand about waiting for a leader while just Stiffing and jiving about what should and could be. Look at us, last count, I believe we got, I know we have thousands of members, but we ain't out here fighting God's fight because all we do is make each other feel good for a couple of hours on Sundays then continue to stiff and jive.

"You know that what I am saying is true. I am thankful that in attendance here are many of our fine political leaders, but they alone cannot stop the crime, the child abuse, neglect, the hunger, the dope dealers, the prostitutes, and all of the others that cause our very streets to be no more than battle, combat zones! BUT! Until we, God's children stop Stiffing and jiving and get their hands a little dirty, their knees scrapped a bit; or even a bloody nose every once and awhile, our streets will remain a battle zone with Satan himself in charge!"

Michael smiled. "I know that the deacons here may be a little nervous, thinking maybe, I have lost my mind. Many of you may feel that I should be talking, saying, preaching about ROY. He was my son and my wife and I will love him forever! But he is back in God's hands now. I know that he is all right! Could be he is wondering what all this fuss is about?"

Michael paused, looked around, "I know that I am not the first one to say this, but I am sick and tired of going to or preaching funerals for our young men and women. Cut down in this spiritual war by the master of deceit, lies, nullification, and death. Starting, right now, I in the name of God Almighty am declaring war against him and his legions of demons. But first, I must confront his two front line generals whose headquarters are in my heart and soul. These generals' fear and doubt are going to have to find someplace else to live.

"Now!" He stopped and looked over the congregation. Many felt that he was looking right into their eyes, their souls.

"Now! I can not speak for another man, woman, or child in here, but starting immediately after we bury Roy in the morning, I going to be out there! Out there fighting the fight for our God Almighty! Whenever, a child needs somebody to talk to, I'll be right out there, whenever, there is a drug user, dealer who wants to find a way out of the vicious circle of crime and punishment and punishment and crime, I will be there! I have had it with Stiffing and jiving with the Word with the Truth, I'll be out there!

"Don't you dare stand up yelling and screaming, Stiffing and Jiving when I ask you a very important question. Pray and think about it before you respond. God's army needs some troops who are ready to hit the streets, stop, Stiffing and jiving, playing church, playing Christians, playing warriors for Christ. Will you join me?"

The affirmation from the congregation was so loud that it must have shaken the very foundations of Satan's domain.

"But, but, but!" he began over the very loud adulation, "It ain't about how much noise...oh! Be it a joyful noise for the Lord, but what you and I do when the crowd is not with you. When you are faced with the choice of doing some good when it is just you and your Lord facing evil! That is when we need to rely on...THE LORD IS MY LIGHT AND MY SALVATION... WHOM SHOULD I FEAR?"

The congregation became frenzied with the notion of kicking Satan's butt!

"I believe God's army needs a, a, a, uh, theme song, he began singing.... 'I sing because I'm happy ...I sing because I'm free....'"

As most joined in singing, Marcus was sitting between his grandfather, Jacque, and Chris. He was peeping at the woman who met them at the door. His grandfather had introduced them to her. Ms. Violet was pretty, no more than just pretty, Marcus knew of no word to describe her charm, her elegance and grace. He was ashamed of the fact the he was surprised that his grandfather even knew such a woman. She spotted him peeping at her and winked at him. He turned to say something to Chris, but Chris was standing singing to the top of his lungs along with the youth choir who were singing an upbeat hymn that he was not familiar with.

After the service, it seemed to take forever for them to reach the church door where Reverend Govans and his wife spoke to, shook hands with, and hugged as many people as they could. Marcus was proud of the fact that the reverend took time away from the other people to speak to his grandfather and the three of them separately.

Jacque walked away from the church holding Ms. Violet's hand. Marcus and Chris followed close behind. Chris was a virtual chatterbox, but Marcus' attention was on his grandfather's talking and laughing with his lady. He had never thought about his grandfather having a girlfriend; and certainly, not one like Ms. Violet.

They stopped as they reached a long, shiny, black, new looking luxury automobile. She handed Jacque the keys. Jacque seated her first, then the boys in the back seat of it that had the unmistakable smell of a new automobile. Marcus felt good and important riding in it, as did Chris. The soft jazz sounds emulating seemingly from everywhere was just loud enough to prevent Marcus from hearing what they were saying in the front seat.

Arriving in the projects, the lady got out of the automobile first. She looked around with a look of exhilaration. As they turned the corner before their home Chris who was walking in front of Marcus stopped so suddenly that Marcus stepped on the back of his shoes.

A small crowd was watching Goldie pitching a fit at his front door. She was cursing, cussing, and fussing while kicking the door of his darkened home. The front windows had not escaped her fury, as they were all broken. The screen door was now busted and she was operating on the door. Chris was scared to death. He looked back at Jacque for protection.

Marcus looked back at Ms. Violet who seemed to be biting her bottom lip. Before Jacque could react, she stepped between the two boys and called Goldie by name. Thinking that it was perhaps Dora, Goldie spun around with the look of a homicidal maniac in her eyes. Goldie seemed to strain her eyes to focus on Ms. Violet. The crowd became excited, as they knew that a fight was in the brew.

Jacque, knowing the oft-volatile Goldie, attempted to step in front of the lady; however, she gave him a quick smile and walked quickly and deliberately towards Goldie. Marcus wondered how long it would take Goldie to dismantle this lady and was ready to jump to her defense while wondering what his grandfather's problem was.

When she got about five feet from Goldie, she began very calmly, "Goldie, Goldie, What in the world is wrong with you?

My friends and I have just left a funeral, and we just do not feel like, not in the mood for all this nonsense. Now, maybe, the party... is just not home and..... (She looked at the door and smiled)... Don't tell me that you and.well; you never know...Why don't you attend to your business later?"

Goldie lowered her head and mumbled something inaudible. She looked at the crowd, then Violet's companions, stomped her foot and stormed away. The now smiling Violet called after her, "Now, we are going to have to talk real soon."

It may have been Marcus imagination, but there seemed to be a look of fear on Goldie's face. Neither Jacque nor Chris noticed as Jacque was holding the frightened Chris.

Once inside, Violet answered Jacque's unasked question, "Oh! Goldie is just a big child. Always has been and always will be. You just have to be firm with her."

Chris heard himself ask, "Well, how do you know her?"

"She was my sister - in - law."

Jacque quickly interjected that Chris was Dora's son. Violet never changed her expression as she scrutinize Chris carefully, "Like they say, it is certainly, a small world."

Jacque reminded the boys that the next day was a school day. He invited them to get themselves a little snack and that he would be going out for a cup or two of coffee. Violet hugged the boys promising to see them soon. Marcus smiled proudly as the two departed. As they stood in the doorway watching them leave, Virginia and Sonia were heading to their home from the funeral.

Marcus heart went out to Sonia as she was still crying with her mother doing her best to comfort her. He wished that he had the nerve to run over to her and hug her and tell her that everything would be all right, while Chris was exclaiming that he was now very hungry.

Chapter 10
Pride

Violet laughed openly, naturally, and loudly. Suddenly, she giggled like a young girl. Jacque could not recall having as much fun. As they continued across town toward the business district, Jacque was not sure where they were going, however being with the effervescent Violet made their destination irrelevant. In the middle of telling him a very naughty and humorous joke, she continued to direct him to the high rent district of downtown where only the rich and wealthy played. He was obviously impressed as they glided into a driveway under the snow white and gold canopy. As she checked her makeup, Jacque waited patiently for the automobile in front of him to be moved while figuring out what to do. Smiling, she asked, "Have you ever been here?"

"Counting today," he laughed, "never!"

"Well, let's go in and see what the chef can whip up for us I am famished" she smiled, kissed him on the cheek as a huge, muscular, white parking attendant broke out in a dead run toward them. She gazed at the attendant while shaking her head impatiently. The man began to apologize, but she stopped him, "we are just going to have to do better. Understand?"

Perplexed, Jacque asked her if she came there often. She responded, still gazing at the attendant, "I guess not enough. Let's go in."

As Jacque reached to open the door, the very huge doorman, attired in a white and gold tuxedo, opened it and spoke to Violet with the esteem often reserved for royalty. He looked like the typical mobster bouncer. The man scrutinized Jacque very carefully as Violet introduced Jacque instructing him "to treat this gentleman as you would me whether he is with me or not."

As they entered the white and gold lobby, there were several other parties, attired in formal eveningwear, waiting to be seated. He could see others seated at the plush, white and gold bar. Jacque felt a bit self-conscience in his off the rack special. Most of the patrons seemed to be extremely pleased to see and speak to Violet. He was stunned as she greeted many of them by name, and totally shocked as she introduced him to many of them as her date. The gesture made him feel very important and proud.

The maitre' d quickly but politely maneuvered his way through the crowd who was waiting to be seated directly to Violet. After exchanging greetings, he led them to what appeared to Jacque to be prime seating. Many of the patrons smiled, greeted, and waved at Violet. As they were being seated, she looked around at the half empty dining room, "Now, will you please go out there and seat those people?" The obviously nervous maitre' d, bowed, said something inaudible to Jacque in French and hurried toward the door.

Jacque had never experience the grandeur of this formal dining room with its lavish white and gold decor. As he was about to speak, he almost choked as he observed one, then some other waitresses who were dressed in white and gold. They were the most gorgeous Black females he had ever seen. Violet laughed, playfully asking him to take his tongue off the table.

"You, uh . . ." Jacque began, but was interrupted by a server that was so attractive that she looked almost surrealistic. She placed a white bouquet in front of Violet and stood there smiling at Jacque.

"Wine?" Violet asked Jacque as she scrutinized the room, looking pass the exquisite creature.

"Thank you." Jacque responded, not able to take his eyes off the waitress.

"Narcissus," she smiled.

"Excuse me?"

"'Narcissus' is the name of this lily and the lounge and restaurant. Exquisitely naughty, isn't it?"

"How is it that I feel that I'm on page one, and you are on page 350?" Jacque asked.

"What do you mean?" she countered as Jacque was being offered a bottle of wine with a gold and white label NARCISSUS'. As he sampled the wine, he laughed saying that she was always ahead of him. She replied with a naughty smile saying she was ". . . just a poor, old fragile thing trying to find a little happiness." Violet insisted upon ordering dinner and he nodded as the waitress reappeared. She introduced Jacque to Naomi and told her to treat him well. Violet added that if he ever brought a woman there to serve them the most scrumptious poison that she could find. They all laughed politely.

"Just tell them back there to throw a little something together for us," she smiled. Then turning to Jacque, "Pretty Is she not? But rather lethal, her last two boyfriends are no longer with us. Now, you were about to ask me about something?"

Jacque told her that she was incredible. She responded by saying that she was just 'fortunate'. He mentioned the way that she handled Goldie. She responded by saying that soon after she met Rommie, Goldie tried to get a little fresh with her. So, she had to kick Goldie's ass. Needing someone to talk to, he told her about his experience earlier that evening with Dora. She was cool, remotely interested and polite until he mentioned the money.

"How much?"

"I don't know I have the envelope here in my coat pocket."

"Really? You better find a safe place to put it. There are many crooks out here. Listen. I need to make a couple of calls. Please tell me that you will miss me."

She leaned over and kissed him on the cheek. Then she surprised him by kissing him on the lips. Those seated close saluted him as magnificent Violet quickly walked away. Watching her walk totally stimulated him. He was a little embarrassed, as his admiration for her did not go unnoticed.

While waiting Naomi brought the salads, the biggest he had ever seen with a variety of huge, fresh seafood, and crisp vegetables. She looked around the room and advised him to be very careful. This caused him to be concerned and confused. There was something about this whole thing that was not just right, and he started to get up and go home. However, this was too much fun.

He assured her that he would be fine. "But you seem to be so very nice," she said before walking away. And what a walk! He was totally astonished by the way she walked. "Man, she could really hurt something with that!"

It was still relatively early when they left the restaurant. Violet was now driving. Jacque asked her where they were going, and she told him that she could show him better than she could tell him. As the automobile glided down the street, he thought about the feast that they had enjoyed. They had been served much too much for the two of them. The balance was on the back seat. Naomi had looked surprised when Violet asked her to wrap up the uneaten food. She signed the check and would not let Jacque give the young woman a tip, saying that Naomi's serving him was ". . . gratuity enough." Jacque slipped her a ten anyway.

They enjoyed a couple of hours of wine tasting, teasing, pleasing, and love making in her lavish red clubroom. Afterwards, she excused herself leaving him for about ten minutes.

"You should go now to be sure that those handsome young men are rested and prepared for school. (She offered him a set of car keys.) The food is on the front seat."

"I can't take your car."

"Look, you need to leave and you have made me feel so good that I sure damned am not going to mess that feeling up by driving a stupid car. We, I do not use the car you are going to drive too much anyway. Actually, you are doing me a favor. It needs exercise"

"I'll bring it back tomorrow" he offered.

"No, tomorrow will not be good. I will call you. Please do not worry about it." She insisted as she pushed him toward the front of the house while nibbling his ear and whispering naughty little things in it. He stopped to give her his telephone number, but she told him that she already had it.

She kissed him before opening the front door.

Under the bright security lights was parked a white luxury sport's car. He turned to tell her that he could not possibly drive, then park it in his neighborhood, but she blew him a kiss. She then gently but quickly closed the door.

Taped to the steering wheel was a note written on stationary with the NARCISSUS logo.

> *Jacque,*
>
> *I really enjoyed our evening together. Love the way you make love TO ME. Must do it again real soon!*
>
> *XXX Violet*
>
> *P.S. To answer a question that I know you wanted to ask. Yes, the restaurant belongs to me along with a few more businesses around town. I hope that will not interfere with our relationship. I need a strong man like you.*
>
> *XXX!*

Jacque sat in the car in the project's parking lot wondering whether to leave it unattended. He was awakened by the slamming of a car door, which turned out to be a cab with Virginia. Seeing him behind the steering wheel, she exclaimed teasingly, "Damned home boy! There's a lot that we don't know about you! What you got a night job pimping?"

Both laughed. He got out of the car still laughing, telling her that the car belonged to a friend. Admiring it, she exclaimed that everybody should have a friend like that as he fumbled with the key pad. Looking into the sky, she said that she wished that she had a friend at home cooking her a little something to eat as the car announced that it was armed.

"You do, I mean I went out to dinner, and I got some doggy bags that I insist on sharing with you" he said reaching for the bags. "Here, help me carry some of this stuff."

"Narcissus! You been to Narcissus? They tell me that the place got gold floors, and silverware and everything! Eric told me that he went there by himself and spent more than two hundred dollars! Man! You sure too much for us poor folks! What you got to eat? ! We can go to my place, and I need to check on Sonia. She did not take the funeral too well, although I must admit it was the best I've been."

Jacque enjoyed watching Virginia eat almost as much as he enjoyed her free - wheeling conversation. As she got up to get another cup of coffee, she asked him if he had heard about Goldie. He told her that he was there when she was trashing Dora's home. Surprised, she looked out of her window, across the court and said, "Well, it looks' like Dora is going to have to find a new sponsor. Was she? I mean, was Dora home when it happened? Did she beat Dora up?"

Jacque answered very dryly that he was sure Dora was not at home.

"What Goldie done found her another woman?"

"No! She's dead! She came down to the bar raising hell about Dora! Boy! Did she pitch a fit?! Anyway, she got really drunk drunk and decided that somebody had taken Dora to Atlantic City. I don't know how she figured that one out, but she decided to go up there and find her. Well, she stormed out of the door and MAN!

"We heard all these shots, sounded like a real war was going on out there! Man! The bar was crowded, and everybody hit the floor! I got down on my knees and prayed my heart out! Then we heard this loud explosion! After a while, it got really quiet, like it does in those horror movies! But none of those so-called gangsters that hang in there would go out to see what had happened. All of a sudden, the police busted into the bar with their guns drawn ordering everybody to freeze! After they questioned us a little, they told us not to go outside, because it wasn't too pretty! Well, you know how people are, and the police might as well have told them to out there! They could have sold tickets to them nosey Negroes.

"Some came back in sick as dogs! I would not even go out there! Eric came back in there looking like he had seen death in the flesh! He grabbed a bottle of vodka, he doesn't even drink the stuff and guzzled much of it down out of the bottle! He finally got his voice back and told me that he ain't never, even in the movies seen nobody as shot up as she was. Eric said that they must have fired hundreds of bullets at her! He said that there were hundreds of bullets in the wall, and so many shell casings it looked like it had rained them. Then he said that they blew up her car. Some kids that were out there said that they were three or four white guys, but they were not saying nothing else!"

"Boy!" Jacque exclaimed, "she sure pissed somebody off. And you really can't blame them kids."

"Yeah! Well, Eric is seriously thinking about selling that Bar. I'd better start thinking about something else to do. Was thinking about going to school. I'm going to check on that first thing in the morning."

Later, while laying in his bed, Jacque thought about his evening. Being with Violet was sensational, but Virginia was more comfortable. Goldie, he had to admit that she was not his favorite person, but nobody deserved to die like that! Nobody!

Much earlier, Johnny and Deloris arrived at the crime scene simultaneously. The street in front of the bar was overcrowded with police cars, fire equipment, an ambulance, news station vehicles, and a cast of scores of curious folk including many children who should have been in bed. Johnny was amused to see the usually immaculate Deloris wearing an old pair of jeans and a teddy bear tee shirt which made her gold badge attached to her belt look counterfeit.

One of the assistant coroners greeted her by joking, "We can absolutely and without fear of contradiction, rule out suicide in this one." He lifted the blanket to show them what was left of Goldie. It took all that Deloris had not to react to the annihilated body. She turned to Johnny, "My brother, let me make this as plain as posible. Somebody called the mayor, who called the commissioner, who called our chief, who called me to solve this thing quickly.

"All them folks know this thing will never be solved. So I'm going back to bed and you got it. Understand?. Keep me informed. I'm history!"

He watched her speed away as he stood shaking his head. Not noticing her emergency lights were still flashing, and her siren was still wailing. Deloris dared the tears to flow from her eyes.

As the boys were eating their exotic breakfast consisting of salad and omelets stuffed with the biggest shrimps they had ever seen, Jacque promised them another surprise. It was their belief that he was going to get them something special as he, maybe, walked them to school. Marcus wondered about him carrying, instead of, wearing his work uniform but dismissed it.

Jacque stopped in front of the house and asked Marcus to see if Sonia was ready. Obediently and willingly, he ran over while Chris watched silently. A few moments later, the four were walking toward the parking lot. As they reached the parking lot, the shining white sport's car stood out like a light in an abyss, like cool pond in an oasis, like, well, it caught all of the kid's attention. Sonia, who had been a depressed soul, squealed enthusiastically, ". . .that's it, that's the kind of car I want!"

As Jacque watched the kids gleefully run around the car, his otherwise no frills notions of life evaporated into thin air. He was ready to live ". . .the good life!" As if smacked in the face by reality, he was now ready, anxious, and impatient to live better than

". . . the damned projects." He looked at his uniform and mumbled "This has got to go, too! Really! Whatever in the hell it takes!"

Marcus, the coolest of the four, tugged at his grandfather's arm, "You going with us?"

"My friends, we are going in style this morning," he said proudly reaching in his pocket for the keys. He manipulated the key pad. The automobiles make a variety of quick sounds as the lights briefly blinked. Chris and Sonia jumped up and down with excitement while Marcus stood there with his mouth wide open.

Jacque opened the passenger doors, helped the boys to the back seats while reserving the front seat for Sonia. One could have cut the pride and excitement that they felt as they glided pass the unfortunates on their way to school.

As he deposited them at school, Marcus eyed his grandfather, turned away and ran toward the building while Sonia and Chris thanked him for the ride in ". . . his car!" It felt good! As he drove away, the car phone rang. "Hello?" he answered cautiously as he was not sure he should have.

"How are you this morning, lover?" Violet cooed sensuously. "I have been soaking here in the tub thinking about you, making the water sizzle! Let's have lunch together before I leave this afternoon?"

He never felt as insignificant as he did as he told her that he was on his way to work. She paused for what seemed like an eternity, "Well, lover, I must leave here for a couple of days. Meet me at the restaurant at eight Saturday!"

"What do I do about the car?"

"Is it out of gas or running badly or something?"

"Well, no, the tank is full."

"Well, then, drive it, lover! Want to give me a wet one over the telephone to cool me down a little?"

"Yes!"

The exchanged telephone kisses.

"Oh! Lover, do not call any of your women on that phone, you might as well know that I am a very jealous and possessive lady; Though . . . well, you know how it is?"

Jacque laughed.

"Who loves you?" She responded laughing and hung up.

Nadine could not believe her good fortune as she saw the news account of Goldie's death. "Somehow, I always land on my feet," she reflected as she headed for work while the twins were fussing about GOD knows what. She did not volunteer, and nobody asked her for a ride to school. So, she went about her merry way, feeling better than she had felt for quite a while. However, on the way to work the lady deejay played a love song for "that special someone, who might be across the country, across the seas, or even across the street. That special someone that, you know what I'm talking about girls, that someone who makes your imagination, YOUR VERY SOUL, YOU KNOW WHAT I'M TALKING ABOUT! The reason you just want to put your arms around his neck and tell him how you feel! Have mercy!"

Nadine felt tightness in her very soul, as all she could think about was Chris. "I'm losing it! I'm losing it! I'm really losing it!" She exclaimed loudly. "Hell! That boy is too young for even my daughters!"

As a disappointed Chris walked out of Ms. Walker's class, he knew that his favorite color was now yellow. He was disappointed, because he had to leave her class to go to social studies. Yellow had become his favorite color, because Ms. Walker was wearing a yellow suit today. She looked as pretty as a picture, and much too pretty to be a teacher. He even got the chance to get close enough to her to smell her when she called him to the board. She even smelled really pretty! All during the class, it seemed that she was smiling at him. Although in his heart of hearts, he knew that it could not be true, his hope was that she liked him - a little.

His social study's teacher, Mrs., Mrs. something, he did not know or care what she said. She was short, some students were taller, and some especially Sonia was much bigger. She looked more like a student to Chris than some students. Also, she was not wearing classy clothes like Ms. Walker.

The class was almost boring to Chris while they filled out the emergency cards. His boredom lasted until she asked why many students did not like social studies. The girl behind him said loudly, "Because it's boring! " Most of the class showed their agreement by laughing, joking, and cutting the fool.

The teacher waited patiently for the class to settle down before she spoke and Chris noticed that she did have a pretty smile, "I know exactly how you feel, felt the same way when I was your age, but let me tell you what I found. I found out that my life held more possibilities than I had ever imagined. I felt that the whole world was like, well, was what I had seen in my neighborhood, in my school, and in my church. I as a child had dreams, my playmates and classmates had dreams of what they wanted to do when they grew up. But as we got older about your age, those dreams seemed to slowly disappear. Do you know what I mean by dreams or a dream?"

Somebody yelled out, "Yeah, like the one I had last night when I was playing basketball and slam dunked on Michael Jordan!" Others yelled out various dreams. Although he did not share it with the class, the only dream that was important to Chris was hugging and kissing Ms. Walker!

She stopped them by saying that those types of dreams were not exactly what she was talking about. Marcus volunteered that he Thought what she was talking about was things that people wanted to do in the future. The word goal was developed.

To the surprise and delight of the students she began to sing, "He's got a car made of suede, got a black leather top, had it made! But when we go on a date, we go in a box on roller skates. So, what about us? We don't mean no fuss but what about us?"

As she sang, Chris thought about Rommie, Goldie, and the other folk he had seen spending cash and talking trash, all whom were friends of his mother. The teacher interrupted his thoughts, "Now, I know that I do not sing very well. Would be surprised if any of you knew the song that I just messed up, but I am sure that the message is clear. What about us? What about you and me? What about you and me in as far as we are all Black, and often, we wonder what in the world we have to be proud of . . .to be proud of. What?"

Chris could not think of too much to be proud of these days, except Ms. Walker.

"We do not want to feel that we are nobodies. So, we search for reasons to do the things that we are asked to do like go to school, study, and do our home assignments. Why? Especially since It seems that everybody, everybody is telling us that we are nobodies as a people, has never been, will never be. So, why should you and I even try or want to get an education?"

The only sound that could now be heard was her voice.

"I will tell you why, the reason is that you are somebody, we are all some bodies! We Black folk share a common history of kings, queens, doctors, lawyers, conquerors, explorers, soldiers, builders, and mathematicians. Much of what is right in this world is a direct result of our contributions to society. We were the first to do many things that others take credit for doing. This school year we are going to begin on a journey though time to learn about ourselves.

"It is said that if one does not know from where he or she has come from, it is impossible for one to know where one is going."

Many students were ready, for incredible journeys, including Chris.

"We are going to be like family this year. We may disagree even fall out from time to time. However, my goal is for us to learn enough about us that we will be proud even more proud of ourselves than we are now. Pride will be our guide.

"Also, you, that is, this is the last time that I am going to do much of the talking. Every one of you will share things with the rest of us. In that way, you will learn from me as well as I from you. Your first home assignment is due tomorrow . . ."

Now, the youngsters who were, for the most part, on her side were now complaining. It was something about the term 'home assignment' that turned them completely off. She stood there quietly for a moment as they complained.

"Well, as I was saying your first home assignment is due tomorrow. Don't ask me where you will find the answer, I do not know and do not care, just find it. Write a sentence or two telling what race Jesus Christ was when He walked the earth. Also, according to our calendar, what year was he born?"

The entire class except Marcus was at a total lost, did not know the answers and did not have a clue as to how to find them. However, much to their dismay, she stood firm.

On their way to the math class, Sonia was walking with Marcus saying that the homework could not be found. He replied that he would tell her the answer to the second question.

Sonia looked at him as though he was crazy.

"The calendar that we use," he began, "starts with the year that was thought as the date that Christ was born. Therefore, according to that. He was born in the first year. As far as His race is concerned, if you think about what she talked about the answer to that is easy. Just think!"

While Chris was maneuvering his way through his first full day of school, Dora was laid back in the tub filled with a bubble bath in a modestly expensive hotel, sipping Champaign and snorting cocaine while contemplating her next move.

Jacque had totally enjoyed his drive to work. Never in his life had he received as many accolades, smiles, and gestures of obvious appreciation as he did as he glided through the streets. But when he arrived at his post, a deserted factory, all those feelings seemed to evaporate in the hot morning air. As he was locking the car, he noticed that on the key chain, what he had assumed was a charm or something was the car's security system remote. He pressed the button, and a deep voice emulated from it, "Warning! This vehicle's security system is now armed!"

After relieving old corporal Pike, a white man about seventy-five, who never found it necessary to speak to him. He changed his clothes in what was the office. He began his first tour of the building. His first thoughts were those of regret. If nothing else, his experience with Violet served as a reminder that he had not done much his life. Certainly with all the knowledge he had accumulated through the years, it would not have taken too much effort for him to be more than a security guard working in a lifeless, empty factory. He thought of himself now as a contradiction to everything that he claimed to believe. This situation was bad enough for him, but he was saddened as he now realized exactly what was he really teaching his grandson.

Deciding that he was going to make a change, he began to think about the two ladies that he was beginning to like a lot. His laughter echoed throughout the desolate building as he thought of all of the material advantages he would enjoy if he were to get really involved with Violet. On the other hand, he was amazed at how comfortably talking to Virginia was. Although, he had no physical contact with her, he felt that loving her would be easier, much easier than it would be with Violet. Love? How long had it been since he had even considered loving a woman. Now, there were two.

Suddenly! He heard the unmistakable scrapping, and screeching at the front door! Alarmed, he reached for his gun but put it away as he heard the voice of his supervisor, Bill.

He could tell that the man was angry about something, but because of the echoes in the building could not quite make out what he was saying. He called out to and walked faster toward the man.

Jacque's supervisor was a young man, but an old style redneck and really did not even try to hide it. Even on those rare occasions when he did bother wearing his uniform, he always wore a cowboy hat and boots. The man also had a confederate flag proudly adorning his pickup truck. To make matters worse, he had the job promised to Jacque, but he was the boss's son - in - law and needed a job. So, Jacque was promised the very next promotion.

"Jesus Christ Jacque! Don't you people ever do any freaking thing right? Damned it all, what we pay you for? Here, come here and explain to me why I had to call the freaking police? What you blind or just another lazy . . .?"

"Lazy what?" Jacque responded defiantly.

Bill, chewing his unlighted stub of a cigar, walked ahead of Jacque with demeanor of a dictator, "Well, sir, you just come out here and explain this here to me."

"What?"

If looks could kill, there would have been a double homicide by the time the two men reached outside of the factory. Two patrol cars on the lot, and another two or three on the way met them!

As if somehow invisible, the officers began to ask Bill about the car.

Bill, now much braver began, "'pears like one of them good for nothings done stole that their car and dumped it here while our boy here was in there goofing off! We doing our level best to get some of them govment contacts, and we got this, person, stabbing us in the back. And we pay the good for nothing good money."

Forgetting that he still had the gun in his hand, Jacque raised his arm to object to being called a boy by this redneck. For his effort, he almost got himself shot by the police!

As the climate calmed, Jacque explained that he had driven the car to work.

"Well," Bill snorted, that solves the damned crime, our boy here drove this fine automobile to work today, because he did not feel like riding the bus, the same damned bus he rode every since he started working here! Where you gonna get a fine automobile like this from, boy. I know how much you make and this car cost what, 70 - 80 thousand or more?"

"It belongs to a friend," Jacque responded dryly.

"A friend?" Bill laughed, where you get a friend that can afford that car! Boys (now looking at the police), I think that we done stumbled on something down here!"

As the police took the gun from Jacque, and placed him in the back seat of a patrol car, Bill strutted about the parking lot as if he had single-handedly captured Al Capone. Soon, they were joined by his benevolent employer John, who was very "Disappointed with Jacque." He assured the sympathetic police that he had no idea," The now sizable gathering was joined by Deloris, who was talking to one of the officers, trying to figure out what was going on. Jacque overheard her advising the officer that had cuffed him that she certainly hoped for his sake that the car was stolen. His partner attempted to explain. About then a city tow truck appeared on the scene.

"No report of it being stolen? Do we have a confession? No? Well, why in the hell did you two geniuses arrest him?" she screamed. "You'd better take your butt over there and release that man! Damned!"

The officer began to continue, "We just could not confirm anything . . . you know how them computers are."

Deloris took a deep breath and asked calmly, "Now, can we assume that the man does not have a valid driver's license and registration?"

Before he could answer, a black luxury car sped toward them. Out of the passenger seat stepped two well-dressed gentlemen, one Black and the other an Oriental. The younger Black man look around, wondering aloud what was going on. The other asked who was in charge. Realizing that the situation was about to become a lot more complicated, Deloris informed them that she was the supervisor. She added that they were in the early stages of an investigation.

The Black man asked what they were investigating. The other walked quickly over to the tow truck driver and stood between him and the car, preventing him from hooking it up.

Violet was visibly upset as she jumped out of the suv! She declared loudly that she hoped that neither her car nor her man was injured. She walked deliberately toward Deloris waving her arms, What is this shit?"

After Deloris assured her that there was an ongoing investigation. Violet paced the lot until she spotted Jacque in the back of the patrol car. Jacque, all but forgotten, was still caged in the patrol car out of her sight.

Deloris knew full well that somebody was going to catch it, and she was not about to take the fall for anybody. She explained that she was called on the scene as there was according to the first officers reason to believe that the automobile had been stolen and since it was an extremely expensive vehicle, it was felt that a supervisor needed to be on the scene.

Knowing that she needed to word what she was about to say carefully, "The officers decided to, uh, detain the . . ."

Violet fully understood what Deloris was attempting to do and asked almost casually, "Was my car parked or . . .?"

"It was, I suppose, exactly where it is now."

The older attorney intervened, "So, as far as you know, Ms. Johnson could have parked it here or left it here while waiting to have it serviced or picked up."

"Yes"

Bill, who was standing there, proudly volunteered that he was the one who caught the thief and had him locked up.

"Locked up?" Violet exclaimed loudly.

Deloris seeing, her career floating away lowered her head speaking very slowly and deliberately, "please get that gentleman out of that car. Also, I want a report from each of you on my desk before I get back to the station."

Violet, still calm but visibly angry, "You are telling me that my man was locked up in that, that pigmoblie, because I lent him my car?"

Silence.

John, Jacque's employer, snatched his hat off his head and stumped it! He looked at his brother - in - law and punched him in the face, fired him on the spot, and told him to leave the truck.

Bill walked towards him to offer him his paycheck which had been his only reason for being there in the first place.

Jacque glared at him with more hatred than he knew that he was capable of having for a human being. Bill tried his best to apologize, still offering him the check. Violet whispered to one attorney, while Deloris and the others watched silently.

"Take it and tear it up," Violet said softly.

The only thing that Jacque wanted to tear up was still and the fool who had cuffed him.

"Take it and tear it up, damn it!" she screamed.

While Jacque stood frozen in his anger, the attorney that Violet had whispered to offered Jacque a position with his law firm. The other walked toward John.

As Jacque tore up the check, the attorney advised John that he would be hearing from the firm soon. He also asked Deloris and the detaining officer for their badge numbers, advising them that a formal complaint would be forthcoming as Violet hugged Jacque.

Still in the tub as high as she could be, Dora suddenly jumped out of it with suds flying everywhere, and bolted toward her pocketbook where she whipped out her telephone book and frantically search for a number. Lying on the bed still very wet, she smiled very confidently as she began to dial the telephone.

She began to make the call but hung up! As she was dressing, she recalled a hotel that she had been to with Rommie. That will work," she said to herself.

At the desk of the hotel, she responded, "No, I have cash! Three-day minimum? Yeah! How much did you say? My name?..........."

The clerk assumed that she was a singer or something, but did not recognize her name. "Should I know any of your work?"

"You working my nerves, I can tell you that,"

Seeing her expression, he quickly abandoned his questions..

"Do you have any other luggage?"

Nodding to the bellhop, "Fine! This gentleman will show you to your suite."

Chapter 11
Miss Scott

Dora indulged herself with a long, hot shower. She slides on a sheer black gown, and slithered across the huge over-sized king-sized bed. It was about 95 degrees outside, but the air-conditioning made it about frigid in her lavish suite. The warmth of her drink as it oozed down her throat warmed and thrilled her. She leaned over to the side of the bed, pulled out one of those "good ones" out of her purse, fired it up, and inhaled deeply. The love song from the radio frustrated her. She tried to remember a love song that meant something to her. There was not one damned one.

She glanced at the telephone for a brief moment, trying to think of someone to call. But who could she call? Nobody ever wanted to be just friends, he or she, all men, women, wanted to have sex with her. Why didn't they understand the sex was not that important? She stood, looking at her reflection in the huge mirror.

"Not bad," she purred. "Damned, it was not always like this. People used to like me, just because . . . You know, I almost wish I were ugly."

She laughed, "Hell no! If I were ugly, I would be on some damned job, working myself to death, raising hell raising children, and having some no-good husband that I'd have to pop a cap in every once and a while. I would have a jive, good looking, broke boyfriend that keeps asking me to leave my no-good family, and dirty, loud barking dog."

"Yeah, they used to like me. Like when I was in elementary school. We used to have so much fun with Miss Scott. She was young and pretty looked a lot like me, and she acted like one of us. She talked kinda funny, because she came from Philadelphia. She used to read us stories, bake cookies for us, plays games in our little one room school, and have so much fun on our little private playground."

Dora pulled up on her "good one" again, and finished her drink. After another long drag she placed it in the ashtray and rolled over on her back. She could almost, no, she saw Miss Scott's face. Miss Scott was always laughing, and called her thirteen students her uneven dozen.

The tears flowed down her face as she remembered Miss Scott dancing with them on the playground on that horrible day. They danced in circles! Smiling! Laughing! Singing!

The tears flowed faster as she recalled Miss Scott's face change and started screaming to the children to run! Run! Run! Dora didn't know what to do, but she heard a loud noise and shouting from behind her. Dora turned and saw an old dirty, yellow pickup truck speeding toward them! As it got closer, she could see three big, long guns pointing at them!

Everything now seemed to be moving in slow motion. The dirty yellow truck began circling Miss Scott and the now hapless Dora. The three in the back, shouting and waving their pistols and shot-guns were wearing white robes and hoods. Miss Scott ran over to Dora and begged her to run, but Dora could not move.

Through her tears, Dora recognized the driver. She could see his face clearly and knew he was deputy-sheriff, Mr. Bob. He spent a lot of time at her father's garage and was her father's friend. So, for a brief moment she thought it was some kind of strange joke.

The swirling dust from the wheels of the truck along with ex-haust fumes and the taunting of the men and the honking of the horn was more than Dora could stand. The screams of her teacher and the sight of the guns caused Dora's head to spin until she fainted. As she slipped into darkness, she saw the truck stop. The three men in the back of the truck grabbed and threw the struggling Miss Scott into the back of the truck.

One of the men threw the gun in the back of the truck and walked toward the cab. He immediately started yelling at the driver! "You damned idiot! Why in the hell don't, you have your . . .?"

Before he could finish, Mr. Bob yelled back as he jumped out of the truck, "Damn it! If ya' ever tries to drive with one of these things on! Hell I could have kilts all of us. I can't sees shit! Next time, Big Henry, ya' drive!"

Then he lowered his head muttering, "Jesus Christ."

Totally disgusted Big Henry yelled, "why in the hell don't you just call the damned NAACP and the FBI, and tell them what the hell we are doing? Now, you know what we got to do!"

He snatched the deputy's pistol and aimed it at Dora.

"Wait! Don't do it! That young, pretty thang done passed out before she could see shit! I was looking right at her ass fall to the ground. Look at her, she pretty enough to give a man pleasure for years. Now tell me. Ya' wants that dead! If she done seed something, I'll put a bullet in her head myself."

"A damned Southern gent is what ya' is . . .!" Big Henry laughed as headed for the back of the truck. As he jumped in it, he helped his companions grope and fondle the struggling Miss Scott.

"Well, Miss Scott, you'd best stop all that fuss," he said calmly, "we are going to teach you a lesson on coming here and messing up the heads of our young niggers. You best just calm down 'cause it is likely that last thing you are going to do is pleasure us before you go meet your Sweet Jesus."

At the same time, Mr. Bob (now with his hood on), was gazing down at Dora, "Look ya' young pretty gal. I don't know if ya' saw anything or can hear me. But ya' tells, I will kill ya' whole damned family and burn that house and garage to the ground. Ya' hears me?"

He kicked Dora's leg just hard enough to see if she would move. Although Dora had seen and heard everything, she was clever enough not to move. Satisfied, he walked to the truck and drove off.

Tearfully, Dora watched the truck fade away.

The local newspaper reported ". . . *according to eye witnesses and the coroner's report, Miss Essie Scott, formerly of Philadelphia, Pa. dies heroically while saving her students from a pack of wild dogs. The sheriff's office reports it had been decided to cremate her body, as it was the only humanitarian action the county could take. It also stated that the quaint little county elementary school would be closed and demolished. Our citizens would never forget Miss Scott as plans were being made to make a memorial park at the site of the old school.*"

There was in the same paper, a seemingly unrelated article. ". . . *Lot #7913 had been sold to a local lumber company. Its new owner, Mr. Big Henry Smite, has promised to give the community's Negro citizens first crack at all jobs to try to heal any misgivings about his company's position as far as race relations are concerned.*" It went further to report that negotiations would be started to make the only local Negro mechanic's company in charge of maintaining all of the company's equipment."

Deputy Bob, while talking to her father, looked straight into Dora's eyes, he smiles, "I know ya' proud of ya' late teacher."

Expressionless, Dora walks away, hearing the deputy, "Lord knows I wish I'd been, there, things would have been very different, yes siree they would have. Anyway, I came pass here to show ya' this here story about ya' taking over all the mechanic work at the mills. Damned, I told ole Big Henry ya' were the man and damned if he didn't' do it. I sure hope ya' hire ya' self some white boys. My lazy-assed son-in-law needs a job before I chunks his worthless ass in the branch for 'gator feed."

From time to time, ole Bob would find Dora on a road walking alone. He would remind her that she was responsible for the safety of her family, even hinted that her Daddy's business would be in deep trouble if she didn't go along. After, the first few times, he didn't have to say much, he would just reach back opening the back door and take her off.

Later, she became pregnant and told him. He told her to find herself a light-skinned Negra, give him a little bit and blame it on him. He drove her to one of his favorite spots down by the branch. They sat under a tree and drank the shine. She drank it to kill the pain of being with him and his nasty kisses, and stinking body odors. This had gone on for much too long, and she thought she was about to lose her mind.

He became extremely agitated, and the shine did not help. The 'gators gave him an idea as he was feeling that he could no longer trust Dora. He told Dora he was gonna kill him some 'gators and ordered her to go to the cruiser to get the shotgun. As she was returning, pointing it in his direction, he began to laugh, "Now, if ya' was a white gal, I'd be a little bit concerned, ya' see. I would be thinking maybe she would blow my brains out and let the 'gators get me, but ya' is my personal colored folk b. . . ."

The blast of the shotgun caused the birds to noisily scatter. While the 'gators were enjoying their feast, she smoked a cigarette and toasted the bastard with some of the remaining shine. She poured the rest on the seat, put a match to a newspaper and laid it on the seat. As the car began to burn, she began skipping down the road while singing the happy song Miss Scott had taught them. She laughed as she heard the cruiser explode.

On the edge of town, she heard a siren behind her. She turned to face the deputy's cruiser. It was another of the three deputies. He grinned, "Dora, now what ya' doing out here all alone. Do Bob know ya' out here? Get in the car (he ordered as he reached back opening the door)."

"Girl, ya' done growed up to be as pretty as that ole teacher gal that we took off. I sure would like to get some of dat. Bob say ya' really good and ya' really like it. I would really appreciate it if ya' could see ya' self-clear to give me just a little bit. Shit! I ain't gonna say shit to Bob."

Dora looked at his eager eyes through the mirror and asked him for a cigarette. He put two in his mouth, lighted them both and gave her one.

"Ya' got some money and some shine?"

He reached in his pocket and threw some bills back at her. She asked him to take her to where the little park would have been. With all the logging, somehow they simply had not gotten around to dedicating the park. It was now very vacant with only beginning saplings and one tree. This tree was special as it was used in the old days for lynching.

He wanted to do her in the back of the car, but she convinced him that under the tree would be much better. She pulled her dress over her head and he began to take his clothes off. With only his boots on, she told him that she could sure use some more shine. She convinced him that it would be better, if she had some more shine.

Returning, grinning with the shine, he suddenly stopped dead in his tracts. Dora was aiming his .357 at him. "Gal, ya' better put that thing down, before ya' get in real trouble." The first bullet missed, and he decided to charge her. The second bullet dug into his upper thigh and he yapped like a dog. The third bullet hit him in the chest. The rest of the bullets dug deeply into and through his face and head. She stood over him, continuing to pull the trigger of the now empty gun.

She dropped the gun beside him and walked to the car. She poured the shine on the seat and suddenly the seats were ablaze. The car exploded as she skipped away laughing! She had not laughed like that since before they killed her beloved Miss Scott.

The High Sheriff and a deputy along with some volunteers found the missing Bob's burn out cruiser. They concluded his drunk ass had set his car on fire and staggered out in the branch where the 'gators got him.

Meanwhile, the other dead deputy was found as the fire had attracted a local truck driver who in turn called it in and departed. The deputy sped to the scene, sneered and snickered at the body.

He saw and took the prized pistol, putting it in his truck before calling the sheriff.

By the time the sheriff got there, people were there including the fire folks who confirmed to each other that the car had burned up and the deputy was dead. The crime scene was totally destroyed by all the folk including the deputy walking around the area, stomping out cigarette butts, and laughing at the expression on the deceased face and his little pecker.

Not to worry, the High Sheriff took one look at his deputy and ordered somebody to put a blanket over his " . . . naked ass!" He knew Big Henry had either killed him or had him killed, as Big Henry was the only one who killed like that. Everybody including the coloreds knew this man had been sleeping with his wife. Although Big Henry swore he had nothing to do with it, the sheriff knew. The coroner ruled it a suicide and since he had no kin, they thought about planting him in an unmarked grave, but they cremated him, as it would be cheaper and done with. By the way, Big Henry beat and stomped his wife for crying when she learned of the deputy's suicide.

Dora's only concern was her unborn child. However, her encounter with her sister's boyfriend settled that issue.

Anyway, while folk were trying to figure out what to do with Dora and her child, Dora was planning to get even with Big Henry. Her father began to complain that Dora treated him with a "long stemmed spoon," only talking to him when she had no choice. He also complained that Dora looked at him "kinda funny like." Her mother dismissed it saying that Dora was really going through some things. Everybody just left her alone.

Dora, overheard her father saying that Ole Big Henry was so cheap that he worked alone on Saturdays and Sundays, because he didn't want anyone to know how much money he was making. He said that sometimes he had to knock and knock on the door of the old two-roomed trailer before Big Henry would open it. On Thursday, she went to his office to ask for a job. She wore a white shorts set. He asked her what she wanted to do.

"It sure gets hot here in Georgia," she began seductively, taking off her blouse to reveal her bare breasts, "Since you the boss, anything you say."

"What about your Daddy?"

"He already got a job with you," she said licking her lips.

"I see, um, why don't you drop pass Saturday afternoon?"

Buttoning her blouse, "I can wait, if you can."

They agreed to meet in the early evening on Saturday. They agreed on meeting by the statue at the end of town. Nobody was ever down there, especially in the evening and certainly not at night or weekends. It was the sight of " . . . that trouble in '66."

After they met they talked, drank shine, beer, and smoked down at the branch, Dora got to kind of liking him; even though, she hated his ass for what he had done. In the background, they could hear the untamed.

"Good damned thing we in this car," the very red and drunk Big Henry began, "those 'gators sometimes walk around here like they are in one of them there malls." Dora was looking out the window, not really paying attention to what he was saying. She was trying to figure out a way to kill this old redneck bitch.

Out of nowhere, he shouted at her, ". . . this where your boyfriend got it?"

"Boyfriend?"

"You know what I am talking about, Bob! Is this about where the gator got him, and his patrol car got burnt up?"

"How in the hell would I know? ... That was white folk's business!"

He gazed at her angrily, pulling her by the hair, "You did kill them boys?"

"What? Who me? Why you want to . . .? Let me go! That hurts"

He laughed aloud, knowing that she could not have the brainpower to figure out how to kill two good ole boys. "Jesus Christ!" he laughed out loud! He reached down and unbuttoned his belt. "I'm going out there to piss, and when I get back, we gonna talk about the damned job. Give you one of them backseat interviews."

He got out of the car laughing as he thought " . . . back seat interview" was about the funniest thing he'd ever said or heard.

Now the hungry old 'gator was in the mud behind a tree waiting for an animal. He heard the door open, and the laughter. He could see the human thing get out of the car, closing the door and walking toward him. As the human thing stood there with his back to him pissing, the old 'gator made his lighting fast move. Dora heard him screaming, and immediately knew that the 'gators done got his ass! She only regretted that she did not see the expression on his face as he was being eaten by the 'gator.

Driving back to town in the cruiser, her only regret was that she didn't' gets any money. She left the car at the statue with the motor running, walked home, and crawled into her window. Her mother had long since gone to bed. Her father's television was watching him sleep. Neither wanted to bother Dora as she was in one of her moods. Nobody knew she had gone out!

The remaining deputy found Big Henry's car with the motor running. He figured that Big Henry was nearby in the bushes pissing. After calling out for him and searching the area for him, he laughed as he thought that he had gone off with one of those fancy girls from down the bottom.

He got in to turn the motor off. He changed the radio station, wondering aloud why Big Henry was listening to Negra music. He moved the car to a safer place. Satisfied he had done a good deed, continued his patrol.

The next morning, totally unconcerned, he told the sheriff about the car.

"Why didn't you call me?"

"I suppose to call ya' every time Big Henry goes off?"

"Is the car still there?"

"I don't know, I guess by now he is finished his business and gone home."

"Let's go see!"

"I'm tired. He can take care of himself. He don't need my help."

Shaking his head, the sheriff asked the deputy to go with him as a personal favor to see if the car was still there. They brought the car back to the station, where it would be safe. The sheriff laughed to himself when he thought about Big Henry returning, looking for his car.

After, a couple of days, his wife called to ask if they had seen Big Henry. The sheriff, knowing that Big Henry had gone off with one of those fancy girls lied, saying that he had to go to Atlanta on special business. He told her that Big Henry told him to watch out for his wife while he was gone. She slammed the telephone down knowing full well that the pig wanted to sleep with her again. Sleeping with him was the biggest mistake she'd made.

Driving through town the next day, she saw her husband's car parked at the station. Hoping he was there, she went in to get some money. The sheriff again lied, saying that Big Henry had called saying he'd be back soon.

Meanwhile, it had been decided that Dora should go away for a spell to help Avory's aunt for a while in the city. As Dora was being driven out of town, she saw the Big Henry's car being towed.

There would be an article in the paper, *"Prominent Business Man Missing."*

"Enough of that shit," Dora said to herself. She slid off the bed poured herself another drink and smoked another "good one."

Charles was lounging in his tastefully appointed office gazing at an oil painting of a country scene, lamenting the fact that his life was so boring. Although he was professionally secure, financially comfortable, and had many trappings of success, he felt empty, alone, and bored with his life. His life generally consisted of getting up in the morning, preparing for work, driving to work, and back home. Boring.

The ringing of his private line interrupted him. His first inclination was to let it ring and deal with it later. However, he answered it anyway.

"Hey handsome," the sultry voice began, "how are you doing?"

"Very well, thank you," he responded not recognizing the voice.

"Well, I bet you never thought that I'd ever have nerve enough to call you with your sexy self," she continued.

"Well, I . . ." he began slowly.

"You what?" she continued playfully, "You know who I am? You really know how to . . ."

"Dora?"

"Yes, Charles. And how is my favorite man?"

Reminiscing the emotional highs and traumas she put him through in Georgia, his first impulse was to hang up, but he decided to hear her out. Sure, he was lonely, but Dora? He needed her like he needed a hole in his head, but decided to hear her out. Since he was not doing anything else, he thought she might be good for a laugh or two. He thought she was going to ask him for some money. He eagerly anticipated the fiendish thrill of turning her down for whatever the hell she wanted.

Sensing his feelings, she gave it her best shot, "I know you might hate me for what happened in Georgia, but I am kind of crazy sometimes. Just a silly country girl, you know what I mean?"

"What can I do for you Dora?" he asked not trying to hide his disdain.

Undaunted, the effervescent Dora replied, "I'm over here in this big, lovely, paid for hotel room with everything that a man could want. I just got out of the tub, and I'm still very wet."

"Wet?"

"Yes baby. I am wet and very hot! Please come over and cool me off! Come over so that I can show you how much I appreciate what you did for my boy and me. Please come over and I'll be the woman of your dreams."

Led by the intelligence of his groins, he drove toward the hotel, hoping, almost praying that his erotic dry spell would come to an abrupt end.

Everyone had left the parking lot except Violet and Jacque. Violet patiently waited for him to stop pacing for a moment or two. She stopped him by asking, "Why are you putting yourself through all this drama?"

"Drama? I, I . . . all I did was to come to work this morning and all hell broke loose. I been humiliated, hand cuffed, belittled, ignored . . . and you ask me what my problem is? Oh! and not to mention unemployed. I..."

"The hell you mean ? You got not a damned job but a position with more money, more everything. You might even end with that detective's agency, if that is what you want, Man! What else you want? You got me!"

"But . . ."

"But shit! You can go find that white man and if you kiss his ass hard enough, he will give you back your slave, J.O.B., or you can come with me, the one who has fallen in love with you. Jacque, you are going to be a very important man in this town. If you want, you can do those noble things that you talk about. Do those things that you say your people need. Get your grandson out of that rat hole! Step up! Damned you, live, love, be mine!"

Jacque looked at her feeling unsure of himself, lost. He wanted to say something, but the words just were not there. She gently caressed him, and they kissed. Afterwards, Jacque admitted that the prospect of moving ahead was exhilarating, but he wondered if he was ready. He had never considered, certainly was not prepared for all that was happening to him.

She kissed him again and laughed, "You are certainly ready all right!"

Violet was really pleased as he had begun laughing. laughter.

She then reached for and grabbed his hands, "Sweetheart, a major problem with us is that we go through life with an imaginary rearview mirror stuck in our brains. We cannot see the present or the possibilities of the future, because we keep on looking back. If that was not bad enough, we seem to always look back at our personal failures or disappointments.

"All this junk keeps us from being the person we could be, the person that God intended for us to be. So, my friend, I suppose the first thing that you may consider is taking that rearview mirror and throwing it right into the trash where it belongs."

"How long I got?" He smiled.

She stretched out her arms, while spinning around a couple of times like a little girl, "Oh! About ten seconds!"

Jacque was not sure what he was getting into, but whatever it was it sure was better where he had been. Now he could feel his rearview mirror disintegrate. He felt good! Better than he could ever remember. All that tough talk about Black men being great, able to do anything that they set their minds to was coming together for him at long last!

As if the very heavens were rejoicing in his emancipation a gentle, warm, summer shower began to sprinkle him with optimism. She offered him, then placed a small cigar in her mouth. He reached for her lighter. As she inhaled, she thanked him for his kindness. The sweet aroma engulfed him as she strutted to her truck.

At this point and time, Violet watched this man seemingly burst out of his cocoon. Like a Nubian King, he faced the heavens and began singing, ". . . the wind and the rain obey Thy will, peace be still, peace be still."

As he sang, tears flowed from his eyes. He could see his daughter's face in the clouds proudly smiling down at him. He knew that everything he had ever done in life was preparation for this moment. He said a silent prayer, praying for guidance for whatever was about to happen.

Almost in a whisper, "Take your wet sexy self home, dry up and change. Meet me in the restaurant at 5:30."

He leaned in the car, kissed her and agreed to meet her. He did not mind getting soaking wet as he watched her drive away. As he drove toward the projects, he decided that his primarily goal was to get himself and Marcus out of those projects. He decided that nothing else mattered.

Meanwhile at the school, Chris and Marcus were on their way to the cafeteria. Through the beehive of activity, Chris spotted

Mrs. Walker walking beside and laughing with a big muscular man with a too tight tee shirt. Marcus told him the man was the gym teacher. Jealousy jolted through his body like electricity; he decided that he definitely hated the man. Almost in a rage, he ripped open his notebook to check his schedule. Sure enough, next period, he had physical education, Mr. Graves. Damned!

It did not occur to Charles at first that the exquisite hotel suite that Dora was in was really . . . well, how in the hell could she afford it! Really, he knew that she could not, but seeing her stretched out on the couch in the outer room of the suite dressed only with a sensuous smile and a black sheer gown made the issue of money totally unimportant. In fact, he was quite prepared to pay for the suite or anything else, if necessary.

She with catlike movements helped him to take his clothes off, threatening to tear them off! Charles' clothes almost hurled themselves about the room, and in seconds he joined Dora on the couch! They rolled off the couch onto the heavily carpeted floor. When they stopped rolling around, he was on top of her. Just as their bodies were just about aligned properly, his lovemaking capacity ended abruptly.

Embarrassed, he rolled off her while trying to think of something to say to cover his shame. But before he could react, Dora smiled knowingly and led him to the bedroom. She stimulated his virgin nostrils with just enough cocaine. She then led him into the shower where they shared the most thorough erotic experience that he had ever had or imagined began.

In the bed, she gently covered part of his manhood with cocaine, after which, his experience reached a plateau of endurance and pleasure that he never knew was possible. As he rested his completely exhausted mind, body, and soul, Charles wished that the magic moment could last forever. Never knew exactly what love was, but he was willing to take this, forever and ever.

Mr. Graves stool in front of the gym door thinking about the flirtatious Nadine. She knew that he was a married man. Still, after all the years they had worked together, she would jokingly (he hoped) ask him when was he coming over to her house; so that, she could rub his muscles. He would always answer that he would when he got permission from his wife.

Anyway, his class was coming and thoughts of Nadine faded. Once on the floor, the boys looked up at him as he explained the rules, regulations and the fact that they needed uniforms and locks. He, also, explained that they needed to take showers after class, knowing full well that most of the time the showers would be out of service for one reason or...

As usual, some kid asked him to show them how to slam-dunk the basketball. Damned! Again, "Mr. Graves show us how you used to slam the rock when you played pro ball. " Somebody, maybe a father, brother, or classmate had told them that he had been the best ever from that city, until he blew out his knee in his rookie year."

It did not bother him anymore. Now, his hope and prayer was to find a kid good enough to be a pro prospect. In that way, he could live vicariously through that person. Chris, totally unnoticed by the man, glared at him with daggers in his eyes. Chris' vision of him laughing with Mrs. Walker was much more than Chris could stand. In fact, he wished that he were big enough to punch the big muscled gorilla. Chris was totally unimpressed as the man demonstrated several basketball maneuvers and shots. Everyone except Chris was very excited as Mr. Graves began to shake, bake, and slam the rock. Chris knew that the gym was not going to be his favorite place, and that the gym teacher could go to hell as far as he was concerned.

A totally exasperated Jacque flopped down in that beat up chair in his room. He looked around his room with disgust. Everything was old, cheap, and in dire need of burning! Everything that he owned needed to be sacrificed to the gods of poverty and despair. He wondered aloud how he managed to live this way this long. He looked at his closet where most of what could be laughingly called his wardrobe was lynched.

Jacque looked out the window pass his well-kept lawn at some men shooting nickel and dime craps. He glared at the young females watching their heroes gamble for maybe enough money to buy maybe a sandwich, bottle: or maybe, even a fix. Finally, he found some things in his closet to wear that were not too bad.

On his way to the parking lot, some old dude asked him for eighty cents, ". . . so that he could get a little drink." The once compassionate Jacque was tempted to punch the old man in the face. As he drove away, Jacque realized that he now hated, maybe always hated them damned projects and the people. He decided then that he and Marcus could not get away from there fast enough. He was going to use that insurance money to get away from those disgusting projects quickly.

Jacque looked at his cheap watch, 12:25. He needed to talk to somebody. He called Michael from the automobile, which invited him to come pass the church to talk. Jacque agreed as he threw the watch out the window.

Dora smiled as she looked down at the knocked out Charles. She toasted herself with champaign as she knew she had this one hooked. She ordered lunch for two from room service and took a quick shower. Charles was dreaming dreams of gliding over the Sierra's making love. Dora's wet tongue entering his ear interrupted his fantasy. As they exchanged hugs and kisses, there was a knock on the door that startled Charles.

Dora put the frightened soul at ease by telling him that it was only room service. Charles watched as she grabbed a handful of money and walked toward the outer room to the door. He heard the waiter thank her about a million times and the door close softly. He did not realize how hungry he was until he saw the food.

Dora waited until he got up to wash before she threw some money on the bed. He estimated it was maybe $ 10-$20,000. "Where in the world?" he thought as he went into the bathroom, trying not to appear to notice the money. But she knew exactly what she was doing, and the fish was hooked.

As they ate, she told him that she had inherited a lot of money, and had no idea what to do with it. She continued by telling him that she needed somebody to look out for her as everybody she knew, except him, would take cold advantage of her. The seeds that she planted instantly grew into a tree as he figured that somehow he had hit the mother load.

Her feelings were confirmed as he told her that he would do all he could to help her. She was so happy that she had found somebody to watch over her that she showed her appreciation in her own unique way.

Michael scrutinized Jacque's face carefully as Jacque tearfully told him about his plight. He began with Dora leaving Chris with him, his negative feelings about his life in the projects, and the fact that he now saw himself as a total failure. He added that he might be in love with Violet or Virginia, or both. Deeply touched, Michael got up and hugged Jacque.

Jacque laughed, "Does this mean we are engaged?"

Michael responded, "Well, my friend, what are you going to do?"

"How would I know? I thought that you were the answer man."

"All I can do is listen to your plans. Maybe, I can help point out the options you have and their possible consequences. But you know that those decisions are yours and yours alone."

"Man!" Jacque sighed, "I just don't know."

Suddenly, Jacque jumped up and headed for the door. He mumbled something inaudible and closed the door behind him. Concerned Michael followed him to the chapel and called out to him. Jacque with tears in his eyes turned to his friend and asked him if he believed in forewarning.

"Are you serious?" Michael responded as he moved closer to his friend, "that's like asking a baseball player if he believed the fast balls. Yes I do. But, Jacque sometimes I find in my business there are, uh, divine warnings. Some believe we have guardian angels. The only way they may have to warn us is through dreams, visions, and what we sometimes interpret as intuition. Man, I do know you are troubled. I want you to know that I am always here for you. Do you want to talk about it?"

Jacque looked him in the eye, "While, I was talking to you, I suddenly, saw you looking down on me with tears in your eyes. I think you were saying something about us being dinosaurs. Man, I got to go. I'll see you . . ."

"Jacque are you all right or should I . . .?"

"No, I'm fine," he smiled, "just feeling sorry for myself. I'll call you."

"Take Christ with you," Michael called out to the fast moving Jacque.

Johnny had been driving, walking, talking, quizzing people all day trying to find a lead to solving Goldie's murder. Nobody was talking. Some were scared out of their wits when he mentioned Goldie. Suddenly, he saw a familiar face walking down the street. Partly out of frustration, and partially out of fatigue, he drove the unmarked cruiser onto the sidewalk in front of the man dressed in a neat but dated, out-of-style suit and jumped out.

Unimpressed the man, tried to walk around Johnny's damned car.

Sarcastically, Johnny began, "the way to treat a good old friend?"

"Look, man, what you want?" the guy almost screamed.

"How long have you been out this time? You okay? Need some help?"

"Look, Johnny, unless you want a recipe for 1,500 inmates, I cannot help you. I am damned near fifty, fifty! And I done spent thanks to your excellent police work, the last ten locked up. You commissioner yet? Both laughed.

The guy continued, "I done finally got sick of this nonsense, I, WHAT? Come out on the streets, get clean. Start hustling, pimping, partying, getting high, selling shit, then you bust my butt. Last time you busted me, I just bought ten of these damned suits. I know the shit ain't what it be these days, but I'm gonna wear this shit and the others like it til they fall off me.

"Shit! I'm tired of the life. They owe me for taking that last fall for Rommie. Lot of good that did, but you know how love is?"

"What in the hell are you talking about?"

"I know that you are hunting them white boys that blasted Goldie, but they gone. The hit was personal, had nothing to do with business, you know. Look! I'm clean, gonna stay clean and when I get my money; I'm getting the hell out of Dodge! Johnny, I can't go back inside."

The man started to walk away, and then stopped. "Don't sweat it, don't nobody give a shit who did it, you know that. But, if you accidentally find out who did it, go to the feds or you be a dead man."

Johnny watched the guy disappear down the street, knowing that what he had said was probably true.

Deloris, who had been cruising the streets, saw Johnny talking to his cousin and decided to wait for them to finish before she approached him.

Looking disheartened, Johnny wiped his brow, "Damned hot."

"What you talking about, big boy, me or the weather?" she joked.

"Well, ain't anybody talking about this one they are all scared to death. Something big is going to happen out here or somebody has decided to completely take over."

"So?"

"So, we'd better be damned careful out here."

"Well, sweetheart, you just go ahead and see where this thing goes. I'm going to get my hair done. We got a date this evening; we are going to Narcissus this evening. Get dressed and meet me about, oh, 6:30. Tell Tracey that you are going to be late."

"Narcissus?"

He watched her walk away flaunting her desirable body. She had the most brilliant mind of any police person that he had ever met. Her physical appeal, and flirtatious, self- centered, easy going exterior caused many to underestimate her probing mind, her attention to detail, and mind that was like a steel trap.

Some officers thought that the two had a thing for each other. However, the only thing that they had for each other was mutual respect, and she enjoyed working him to death. So, although he had no idea why they were meeting at the Narcissus, he'd be there or he'd have hell to pay.

Chris left the gymnasium as angry as he could be! He did not like the man at all! In fact, if he were a bit larger or the man a bit smaller, he may have tried him. He voiced his resentment of the teacher to Marcus, who liked the man and did not understand what Chris was talking about.

Chris stopped and glared at Marcus menacingly. At that point and time, he hated Marcus with all of his heart and soul! He hated every inch of this dark, lanky, funny talking, African Zulu or whatever he was. Chris felt like smacking him in his damned, ugly face. As Marcus walked ahead of him not knowing that Chris was going through all those changes, Chris ran up to Marcus and banged him in the back of his head!

The speed, natural athlete, and self - defense training which were spontaneous compelled Marcus to respond by whacking his attacker with a lightening fast punch and kick! The force of Marcus, response caused Chris' frail body to slam against the wall lockers. It happened so swiftly that those around them had no idea what had happened. Stunned, Chris looked up at the surprised Marcus. He extended his hand to help Chris from the floor.

With tears flowing from his eyes, Chris screamed at Marcus, jumped up and ran down the hall. Marcus started to run after him to find out what had happened, but a teacher grabbed him. While the teacher was demanding an explanation, Chris was running wildly down the hall. He spotted Mrs. Walker. She was instantly alarmed, concerned, and frightened for him. She grabbed him and attempted to console him, quickly and discreetly.

Tears ran down his face like the River Nile as all of his heartache, disappointment and fears that had built up since leaving Georgia finally came to a head. Not understanding but feeling his pain, she took him into a seldom-used room. She sat in a chair and tried to get him to talk to her. He couldn't. Nadine wiped away his tears with her hands, feeling his tender young skin in her hands.

He began to mumble something about Marcus and Mr. Graves and her, and some other stuff that was incomprehensible to her. Her maternal instincts caused her to grab and hug the boy. However, his wet face and lips against her breast caused a hot flow in her soul. She opened her eyes and glanced at the closed door, while now embracing the youngster. She pushed him away gently as common sense took over. But she then placed his precious face between her hands and kissed him gently on the lips.

Chris had at first been too upset to really appreciate being held and hugged by Mrs. Walker. But now, the gentle kisses made him feel like, like he did not know how he felt except, well great! Her warm, moist tongue forced his mouth open, and the sensation of her in his mouth caused his entire body to float. He felt his own tongue being simultaneously being sucked inside her mouth, which caused him to become rigid.

She placed his head in her hands, gently guiding it in her cleavage. The rhythmic gyrations of their bodies caused a wondrous but strange sensation exhilarating his body and soul, which suddenly caused him to jerk involuntarily. He squeezed her as tight as he could. He felt like he was part of her. Then, like a bolt of ecstasy, his body seemed to explode. He felt a strange as liquid filling his underwear. He felt strangely fantastic!

Nadine felt it much more intensely. Nothing now mattered more than this young boy. She wanted him more than she wanted to breath. She pushed him back far enough to grab his belt. She could see the astonishment and confusion on his face and smiled to let him know everything was all right as she looked around the dark room for a place more secluded, comfortable.

Suddenly, as if an omen, the bell sounded. It was louder than she had ever remembered it being. Almost instantly, the halls were filled with kids who were louder than she could ever remember them being. She realized as much as she wanted this young boy, it was certainly not the time nor place. She released his belt while whispering to him.

Chris was so confused that he could not quite comprehend what she was breathlessly whispering to him. He examined her face that now looked strange. Frightened and confused, he broke for the door. Before she could utter another word, he was out of there!

She whispered, "Chris, its going to be so good!" as she straightened her clothes and prepared to leave the room.

Chris hit the front door like a speeding freight train, but once he cleared the school, he had no idea where he was going. His pace slowed to a crawl as he tried to figure out what was happening to him. As the tears flowed from his lonely eyes, he wished that he could just die, get this stuff over with, and be with his grandmother who truly loved him.

Tempted to run in front of a truck or something, he thought about Mrs. Walker. Somehow, he felt that he had gone much further than she wanted, and he was in trouble. Even if, she did not tell, he could never face her again.

Chris wondered where Dora was, like she really cared. He walked aimlessly toward his home. As he got closer to it, he saw the battered door and window, which reminded him of Goldie and Ms. Violet. He sat on his steps, thinking about how messed up his life was and he could not think of one reason to, to live. He felt again that he would be better off up there in the clouds with his grandmother and father.

Christee was so tired from working those two jobs and going to school that she started not to answer the telephone, but it could have been Chris. On the telephone was Mr. Solomon, who was (laughingly) her agent.

"What you want?" she responded to his cheerful greeting monotonously.

"You are on your way, baby!" he almost screamed.

"On my way to where, Belleview?"

"Funny, well, young lady, the producers of a new movie want you in their next movie opposite a star that I will not even dare to mention over the telephone. Sweetheart, believe me, you are on your way."

"Whom, oh, man I ain't got time for no bullshit!" she exclaimed hoping and praying that he was telling the truth.

"Listen, do the initials "D. W." mean anything to you?"

Christee's heart began to race with excitement.

"Christee, they saw your still photos, your promotion videos, and they feel that you are perfect. They are so convinced that I have a ticket. Oh yes, and some money for you to do some shopping before you go out there. When I met you, I knew that you were going to happen, baby. So, come pass my office, catch a taxi, we will pay. Come on, Sweet heart, sign these papers and get yourself out there and show them what they have been missing."

Christee almost fainted as she thanked him. She hung up with tears in her eyes and thanked God for blessing her. She looked around her shabby flat and screamed, "Good damned bye!"

Jacque was now sitting in the restaurant wrestling with his feelings as well as the drink that he was served. Too sweet! He casually watched Violet sitting across the huge formal dining room. He had been diplomatically seated away from her by the maitre' de in a far corner opposite to where she was seated. She was seated with three men who looked just like they had stepped off the set of a mafia movie. As he was about to give up on his drink and order another, Violet jumped up screaming at the three gents.

His heart began to race as two of them stood up, seemingly attempting to calm her down, while the other sat serenely. One reached for her! She side stepped him and picked up a glass and threw the water in it at the guy who was seated! The water did not miss! Jacque leaped out of his seat and charged toward them!

Even though it was quite a distance, the two men spotted his move. One stood in front of the seated man quickly as he menacingly unbuttoned his jacket! The other rapidly intercepted Jacque with his right hand in his unbuttoned jacket. Violet seeing this, jumped between him facing Jacque.

"You take your ass back over there and sit down," she ordered softly smiling, "don't you ever interfere with whatever the hell you see me doing. You could have gotten your chauvinistic ass ki . . . hurt, causing a scene in my damned place."

She instantly composed herself, kissed him on the cheek, "That was very sweet of you; but, baby, believe everything is fine. Please go and wait. I will join you when I finish with these gentlemen. It is just business."

The guy standing between her and the table buttoned his jacket as he backed toward the table with a smirk on his face. He never took his eyes off of Jacque. The coldness of his blue eyes made Jacque want to go somewhere and hide. The others at the table did not seem to be concerned about the situation one way or another.

Naomi was standing near his table, and he could see what looked like fear maybe concern in her eyes. As he was about to sit, she discreetly maneuvered him to a chair with his back to Violet and her party. She glanced over at the table where Violet and her party were sitting. Seeing that they involved, she whispered to Jacque to get up, leave, and never even look back.

He knew she was absolutely correct, but the macho thing took over and smiled saying, "if you will bring me another drink, I'm fine." she shook her head knowingly and walked away silently to comply with his request.

Distracted briefly by her walk, wondered how it would be if she were to... "If?" he pondered as he fingered his napkin. "If folks in hell had ice water, if this thing kills me, if!" He attempted to make sense of it all.

"If this damned thing kills me, it will be played out!"

Chapter 12
Dining with Deloris

Deloris parked in her cruiser in front of 'Narcissus' much to the annoyance of the parking attendant. She playfully stuck out her tongue at the man and laughed loudly. He walked away cussing, calling her names under her breath in Italian. She looked at her watch 7:42. She was very amused as the parking attendant had to maneuver the patron's cars around her cruiser. She radioed Johnny, "Where are you lover? You know I do not like to wait!"

"I will be at your twenty in five. Can't wait to see what you are wearing!"

"I love it when you talk like that! Hurry Lover!"

By the time he parked behind her car, Deloris was standing on the sidewalk twirling her keys and giving the parking attendant the absolute blues. The parking attendant tried to convince Deloris to let him just pull her car down a little. Deloris and Johnny laughed as they approached the entrance. Once there, the big, muscular doorman eyed them like a cat would watch a canary. "You get all them musculus by opening and closing doors?" Johnny teased. Deloris laughed.

Deloris twirled, "You like my dress?"

"Love it," as they approached the snobbish maitre' d.

"I do not believe we have reservations for you two." He did not know Johnny, but he certainly knew Deloris.

"Oh goodness," Deloris replied, mocking being hurt and surprised.

"Well, is Violet here?" she asked firmly.

"Unfortunately Mrs. Johnson is not here."

"Well, you just be a good old boy and sit us at her table. My feet hurt and you'd best hurry. Understand? I am sure she knows I am here. So, when you call her back, tell her that we are broke and hungry"

He seated them without comment.

Johnny scrutinizes the restaurant meticulously. "You mean to tell me that a Black woman owns this place?"

"Yes, and a real live black widow," she responded dryly.

Johnny choked on the water he was sipping, when the gorgeous Naomi approached them, asking for their drink orders. She added that the chef had already begun their dinner.

"Madame Violet is very pleased you cared enough to dine with her and she will join you as soon as possible. Also, she asked me to remind you that your money is certainly no good here. And she asked me to extend every courtesy to you and your son."

Johnny laughed as Deloris smiled and shook her head.

"Your drinks? May I suggest one of our virgin frozen specialties? We certainly would not want you to be compromised by alcohol. Many of your high ranking officers find our wet bar selections very satisfying."

"We offer two frozen virgin strawberry selections"

"Make it water." Deloris countered

"Cigarette! I need a cigarette! Fast!" Johnny clowned as he watched Naomi's seductive walk, "she just made love to my eyes!"

"Be careful of what you lust for, lover. I would hate to have to lock her ass up after finding you in some dark, dirty hole or alley, maybe dumpster."

As they were talking, elegantly dressed in a pearl while pants suit with gold trimmings, Violet sauntered behind Johnny. She placed her hands gently on his shoulders, "How very good to see you Deloris."

Seating her quickly, "please do not tell me that his handsome young man works with you. He is much too delicious to have a drab job like yours. I ordered my chef to prepare you and your too young for you friend a real yummy treat. He had to send out to China Town for a special spice that I wish you to have."

"Why thank you dear! May I offer for my colleague and myself our deepest sympathy to the grieving widow? I am, soooo happy that you are not wearing drab black. White makes you look so, um, virtuous, angelic."

"Deloris, you could never know how much your condolences mean to me." Gazing at her, ". . . and may I add that you look good in that dress every time I see you wear it. Looks as good as it did five, six years ago when you debuted it. We really need to go shopping someday soon."

"Your drinks," Naomi offered, this time with a glowing smile. She presented them with two elegant looking huge tropical drinks and a glass of champagne for Violet. Violet glared at Naomi, "you know better."

Naomi quickly removed the glass of champagne and hurried away.

Deloris, glaring Violet in the eyes, ". . . we also offer our deep regrets concerning your sister-in-law's untimely demise."

Violet put a cigarette in her mouth and waited for Johnny to light it. Naomi returned with the wine steward. As she approved of the champagne, she thanked Deloris for her ". . . deep concern." Johnny, again, was distracted by Naomi and seemingly paid little attention to the ladies.

Sipping on her champagne, "these are difficult times."

"They may get a lot more difficult, if I . . . well, look at the time. Johnny and I really must be leaving. It was good having this little chat with you. We will have to get together soon."

"You mean the three of us? How deliciously kinky."

"No, Mary. One day it is going to be just you and me."

"Just as well, perhaps while we are dancing, I will be able to convince Naomi to spend some quality time with your young man.

We are both much too old for him, especially, well, I am looking forward."

As they reached the front door, the parking attendant was having an animated argument with a tow truck driver. He waved enthusiastically at Deloris, "Girl friend, they really crazy down here with their want to be mafia looking selves. They want me to tow your car. I ain't towing shit!"

"Love you!" she laughed, but stopped when she saw the white sport's car pull in behind Johnny's. Jacque recognized her. He spoke cheerfully as he got out of the car. Violet came out of the restaurant, whispered to the doorman, who gazed at Johnny.

Quickly, Deloris smiling walked over to Violet, whispering, "Bitch, if Johnny so much as catches a cold! They are going to be putting a tag on your big toe." Violet's smile turned to a scowl.

Still composed, Deloris walked slowly over to Johnny and ordered him in her car as Jacque and Violet drove away.

"You Mr. Investigator, go find that damned Dora! I believe we may get some answers." Before Johnny could answer, "you still here? Go find her! I'm hungry!"

Johnny stood on the curve next to the not too pleased doorman as Deloris sped away.

"You think I can get a book of matches? My wife likes to save matches." The guy completely ignored him.

"I'll get my own damned matches." He walked in the door and found himself almost nose to nose with Naomi. "You come back to question me, officer? Pat me down? Beat me with your big... Violet said you might."

Breathlessly, "I, Oh! All I came back for were some matches for my wife, I mean, friend. Hell, my wife!

She reached behind the stand and handed him a handful of matches. "I always give a man more than he asks for."

Charles looked up from the floor to the bed with Dora sound asleep and snoring. "Imagine that, fine as she is snoring like a pig," he laughed.

He got up poured a drink and walked around the room slowly. His mind was racing! He picked a cigarette off the table and reached to get a match. He laughed to himself, while pondering what he should do. His first thought was to get dressed and leave. But then he thought about the money. Knowing that it had to be dirty, he decided to leave again. But what if it can't be traced? No! Wasn't worth the risk? So, he decided to leave again. On the other hand, he could, maybe, get her to stay there a few days and at least, he would have the sex. But what if somebody was looking for her?

As he slid into the bed, Dora, still sleep, wrapped her arms around him and covered his leg with her leg. Now, feeling good by being enveloped by Dora, Charles felt amazingly powerful. Everything he had ever done, schools, college, honors, jobs, automobiles, the apartment was for one very important goal to him. That goal was to have a fine woman like Dora. Nothing else mattered. He had known from the moment he met her he would do anything to have her like this. How could he make this last?

Dora stirred a little, then slowly slide out of the bed as Charles pretended to be sleep. Returning, she slithered under him kissing his face.

"We have to talk."

"About?" he yawned.

"Money honey," she moved and grooved under him, "you know about money. I want to live like a rich bitch. We will make a perfect pair. I need somebody to watch my back that knows what the hell they doing!"

"I am this person?" running his fingers through her hair and kissing her.

"Yes baby. You are the one."

"And you absolutely trust me?"

Dora laughed, "You ain't the type who would try to rip me off. You so cute, you smart, real smart, like the way you talk, but you ain't got the kind of thug in you that would make you try to flip me. So, I ain't hardly worried about your sweet punk ass." She grabbed his head and kissed him passionately.

Not too sure about being called a ". . . sweet punk ass," but he knew he needed Dora as much as he needed to breathe. The money was merely a bonus! She called room service; she turned on a jazz station, which mildly surprised him. "Well, lover, how are we going to keep me a rich bitch?"

"The first thing we need between us is honesty. Where did the money come from and how much is it?"

"Well, my man Rommie, in a way left me all this wonderful money!"

"Who the hell is Rommie?"

"Was..."

Dora told him all about Rommie, his business, the money, and a few other things that he could have lived a thousand years happily without knowing. It all sounded like a cheap B movie to him. But there she was, the money, and now the delivered breakfast, which he insisted on paying for. While sipping his coffee and examining Dora's eyes, he knew that he was in for the ride! In for good! He laughed to himself, "for better or worse."

Johnny drove back to Eric's, laughing at Deloris. He thought that with any kind of luck, Dora would be there. He could question her; or maybe, lock her up. Then he could go home and with his wife and go to sleep.

The joint was jumping as he entered the bar! They were partying so hard that the jukebox was dancing across the floor. The dancing was wild, funky and furious especially for an older crowd. He laughed as he imagined his wife being in this place with Nadine.

He walked to the bar and was greeted cheerfully by the barmaid. "You are much too cute to be the police."

"And you are too fine for words, but before we get engaged, married, and have children, I need to ask you about Dora. You know her? She here?"

Eric intervened, telling him that he was surely glad the police were there after the night they had. When asked, he told him where Dora lived and armed him with a picture of her from the wall. Close to the end of his shift, he decided to call in and go home. He'd see Dora in the morning.

Laid back in a lounge chair beside her pool, Violet was polishing off her second bottle of champagne. She was so preoccupied that it seemed that Jacque was not even there. At first, he was able to occupy his mind with the music, the gentle waves on the pool, and flickering lights. She looked ravishing in her very thin pink bikini, but she ignored him.

Suddenly, as if out of a trance, "oh Jacque, why are you looking like you lost your last friend? Don't, you like being here, just a little bit?"

"Violet, it is getting late. You look a little tired and may want to go to bed."

"Oh baby. You are so deliciously bad. I loved it when you talk like that! Get so excited." She poured herself another glass of champagne, checked her watch, and again, became remote. Her behavior made Jacque very uneasy. However, each time he suggested leaving, she was not hearing it.

Now, the sounds of the ripples from the pool, the soft music, were now getting on his nerves. Suddenly, the telephone rang! After all the silence, it sounded as loud as cathedral bells to Jacque.

"Hello," she began softly into the portable telephone, then she began to scream, "I really don't care about any of that. You have five minutes!"

He watched her as she bit her bottom lip while gazing at the telephone. She started a smile, and then a grimace, mumbled something, and threw the telephone into the pool.

Having had enough, Jacque stood up determined to leave. She gazed at him and ordered him to sit down. As they made eye contact, he felt a demonic coldness about her. As he slowly sat, he could not decide whether he was surprised, concerned, or just plain scared to death.

The sound of the telephone gave him some relief and time to figure this thing out as she went indoors to answer it. He decided to leave her keys on the table, get the hell out of there, and get home the best way he could. He was, he admitted to himself, very scared!

He jumped as he felt two hands gently grabbing his shoulders! He leaned his head back into the lower stomach of Naomi and looked up at her smiling face. She stood above him smiling and holding his shoulders firmer; "I will not hurt you, if you do not hurt me."

As he laughed nervously, Violet stepped through the door with another portable telephone in her hand. She was now wearing a sport's outfit with a very huge pocketbook. She gazed at the two of them as she continued on the phone, "Okay, your hotel. Right! Sure! No, by my damned self! I'll deal with it myself! Right! It is my money, so, sure!

"Be right there! Love you. I owe you big time."

Her phone rang again, after listening briefly she laughed, "No, I am sure I can handle this. Thanks for your concern."

Violet began to pace, looked down at Jacque while glancing at her champagne bottle. She placed a cigarette between her lips and waited patiently for Jacque to light it. She looked at Naomi, "my bottle is empty." Naomi quickly went into the house, returning swiftly and served Violet.

Violet nodded and told Naomi that the telephone was at the bottom of the pool. Mesmerized, Jacque watched Naomi, quickly disrobed. She was not wearing underwear. She dived into the pool, retrieve the phone and handed it to Violet. She was asked to face Jacque as Violet began to dry her back and shoulders with the sun beginning to rise. Violet laid the towel on a lounge and gently led Naomi to it with her eyes fixed on Jacque.

She picked up another towel and offered it to him, "I am going out to pick up a long due debt. (Smiling broadly) Just look at all this eye candy. Please make sure she is almost (she giggled) completely dry.

"When I get back later, I expect you to be well on your way. Jacque please lends me your car keys." She accepted the keys and quickly departed.

Slowly wetting her lips, Naomi asked him if he was going to finish drying her. Impatiently, she grabbed another towel and began drying herself. He watched her as she walked into the house with that same amorous walk.

She returned with two drinks and a long business envelope.

"Fifty-fifty all right with you?"

He looked at her blankly.

"Shit! You don't, I mean, you really don't know what's up! Lover, I will fill in the blanks, but you done, turned out, flipped! And now you mine, all mine! Remember what I told you in the restaurant?" He nodded.

"Well, you are about to step in deep shit! Or you can walk away! But since you have come this far, walking away can be as messed up as hanging around. Know what I mean? Like one day you will pay. You will pay with your very ass. All of us will"

"My ass?"

Gently leading him indoors to the huge, well-appointed red playroom, she shook her head while laughing softly. In the middle of the room was that huge round red waterbed. She sat him down on it. He recognized the bed and realized that the next few minutes would determine how well and very likely, how long he would possibly live.

"Look around this room. She designed it! See the knives and guns and shit around the walls. All that shit is real and just about everything is red, blood red! Hard and soft but red! I believe she really liked you, but she hates me! You could have lived above this shit, but she thinks you want me.

"She is a very sick, dangerous bitch! She has spit in the face of death many times and will do it again in a heartbeat. She loves that shit! Never forget she is deadly, nothing in the hardware store will kill you as fast as her.

"She expects us to drink like fish, make love like rabbits, and go to the city and pick up some product. While we are there we can party, shop, make love as much as we want and be back in three days. No sooner, no later, she's superstition in the flesh! The money is for our expenses; the product is already paid for.

"On more thing, if it gets ragged, you are to take the fall. She will get you out, but you take the fall. Understand?

"Like I said, my mother is sick, she is jealous of me but could not stand me doing a bit. But don't worry, the chances of getting busted is close to zero. They have ways of concealing that will blow your mind. One time they had a city councilman bring it here, and he never knew, and we sent his jive ass home happy, if you know what I mean."

As she was talking to him, all he could think about was Marcus. He knew that not only would Marcus be messed up behind this, but also everything he had ever taught Marcus would be a lie.

He stood up totally disgusted with himself for thinking he was getting something for nothing. He bent over and kissed Naomi on the cheek, "...it has been, been quite an education. It has been as exciting as you are beautiful. But I'd better go. God knows I'd best be going."

She smiled, "wish I could leave myself, but this is my life. If you ever need anything..."

As he began his long trek home, he prayed that no harm would come to him. He felt like a total idiot taking those risks while being his grandson's only living relative, support, and provider. Jacque felt nothing but shame as he realized what he had risked. Now with his pockets empty, heart broken, and he feeling very stupid, Jacque began to feel a little better as he heard himself singing "Amazing Grace!"

"I can't be there in fifteen minutes," Johnny protested on the telephone, "since you put it that way I will." Tracey, laughing, blew him a kiss as he stumbled while putting on his pants and dressing.

Chapter 13
One Daughter Too Many

The morning air, the smooth humming of her automobile elevated that special exhilaration Violet was feeling which did not happen often enough. Nothing ever made her feel as alive as the deed that she about to do. She laughed loudly as she turned up the volume and accelerated her finely tuned automobile. This was going to be a great day!

She parked across from the hotel and skipped across the street as she was now anticipating having a very exciting and rewarding morning! The high she was feeling was marvelous! Once in the lobby, she walked quickly to the desk where she cheerfully asked for the manager. Before the clerk could answer, he appeared from the back and discreetly beckoned her.

Meanwhile, Deloris and Johnny arrived from different directions and sandwiched Violet's car, however neither paid attention to it. As they crossed the street, Deloris joked that she did not want to face dangerous Dora alone. They unnerved the clerk with rapid badge flashing, and fast-talking. The clerk quickly identified Dora and pointed to the elevator.

Charles had dressed and was about to leave. He assured Dora that he would have a plan for the money very soon, adding that they would have to clean it first. Dora followed him from the bedroom and insisted on a long passionate kiss before he left.

As he waited for the elevator, Charles heart was thumping. He could not wait to get back there with Dora. When the door opened, a lady amused him with a very small dog looking thing getting off as she kissed and baby talked it. Another door opened. From behind he heard, "Pardon me sir, may I have a word with you?"

He smiled broadly as he admired the very attractive woman.

She began, "I, well, to tell you the truth, this is a little awkward my sister is up here in suite 1407. Would you be the gentlemen who, let's say, had breakfast with her?"

As he nodded, he seemed to remember that her sisters looked a lot like Dora and younger. He could have been wrong and was not really concerned.

"Goody!" she laughed, "will you be good enough to go back there with me? I have a big surprise for her and would just love it if you were present. I, for one, would not want you to miss it, and I am sure she would want you to share the, um, experience with her."

Deloris and Johnny stepped another elevator off fussing about football. Immediately, Deloris and Violet locked eyes. Deloris spoke to Charles, "you certainly keep bad company if you are with her?" Nerves shot, he answered, "Yes, I mean, no, I was just . . . she asked me if . . ."

Johnny drew his huge gun, ordered him to step away from Violet with his hands stretched out. Charles fainted. Neither, Deloris nor Violet took their eyes off each other, while Johnny knelt and searched Charles for a weapon. Noticing Violet had her right hand behind her. He flanked the woman with his weapon drawn. Now smiling, Violet began to breathe heavily, "You want me after all? Let's go into one of these rooms!"

Deloris smiled, drawing her baby cannon, "Mary, it is time to play show and tell. Show me your other hand. Let's do it slowly, Mary!"

Violet's eyes danced between the two as Johnny had completely flanked her and was now pointing his weapon at her head. He whispered, "Just slowly raise your hands. I would hate for that outfit to get all messed up."

Violet recalled years ago when Deloris was the lead investigator in the murder of Violet's father, Pickles. Deloris had always believed that Violet had him killed, but there was never enough evidence. It was no secret on the streets that she wanted her father dead. She wanted him wasted as the old fool as he was getting soft. He was short sighted, and did not realize he needed a front for his huge drug business. Although the only child, only daughter he had, she was one daughter too many.

Deloris continued, "Come on Mary! I do not want to kill you, just drop it, but don't take too long. You can easily beat a weapon's charge! Your lawyers will have you out before lunch"

Violet was sure that Deloris would hesitate long enough to get her fired up. But the man, she could not detect any weakness in his eyes. However, she was damned tired of Deloris, always in her shit!

Charles began to stir, and Johnny glanced down at him. Her chance! Her heart began to beat faster, faster! She could do it! She felt that special surge run threw her body as she quickly began to raise her right . . .

There were two very loud explosions! Violet heard neither as her body slammed against the wall, then flopped to the floor on top of Charles!

Johnny lowered his unfired weapon, looking into Deloris face. She looked at Violet's body, then at Johnny. For a brief moment, she wanted him to grab and hug her, but she complained about a broken fingernail. Johnny checked the body and confirmed that Violet was no more.

With the exception of Dora, who was laid back in the tub, smoking another good one, the guests peeped out to see what had happened. The thick smell gunpowder caused many of them to cough and/or sneeze.

Seeing Deloris with her baby cannon in her hand standing over the late Violet Johnson was enough for most to retreat behind their doors. As Charles regained consciousness, he felt wet on his face. He wiped it, seeing the blood, fainted again.

Soon the floor was filled with police, paramedics, a police photographer, and the press. They were all struggling for space in the hallway. Having given a statement, Charles somehow managed to walk down the stairs to his car where he sat behind the wheel, shivering like a leaf. He tried to process what had happened. He knew he needed to go home get a drink, shower, change, and throw the clothes he had on away.

Deloris was now sitting in her cruiser, looking across her hood at Violet's car." It really didn't have to go down this way, Mary." Deloris wept. "I never really hated you Mary. We were just on the flip side of the same coin." She assured Johnny she was fine. She headed to her home.

Naomi was now sound asleep, but sleep did not come easily. She knew that Violet would be mad as hell, and off Jacque for practice. Naomi decided that she would have to pick it up alone. She would have all the money.

Fighting back the tears, Jacque continued to walk. His feet, ego, head, heart, and soul had one thing in common. They all hurt. He could not stop the rain from flowing from his eyes. There was a gentle tap on his shoulders, "Man, I called out to you. Why did you not answer?" Michael began, but seeing the tears, he led Jacque to the car silently.

Jacque took off the expensive shoes that Violet had bought him. He mumbled that they sure were not meant for walking and asked Michael to stop the car. He placed the shoes on a trashcan and laughed.

After a long silence, Jacque shared his experience with Violet with Michael, which made him feel a lot better. Michael listened carefully and silently until his friend finished.

Michael smiled at his friend, "getting something for nothing sure can be expensive." They both laughed.

As they neared the projects, they saw Virginia with two bags of groceries. They stopped, offering her a ride that she gratefully accepted.

"Jacque where's your ride? Your smooth pimpmoblie that . . ."

Jacque interrupted as he turned to face her, "I will not be driving that car, but I will take you anywhere you want to go. Sometimes a man searches the world for a special pearl, but finds that it was always in the oyster in pond across the court from him."

Michael looked in his rear view mirror at the blushing Virginia.

Charles was so scared that he was still in his car shaking.

Meanwhile, totally exhausted Johnny was on his way home to sleep.

Deloris was at the pistol range, acing the targets.

The boys were anxiously waiting Jacque.

Denny was sitting on the curb and saw the three drives by.

And Dora was laying on the bed, drinking and yelling at a guest on a television talk show.

Chapter 14
Why Didn't I Know?

The boys were frying bacon, eggs and making toast while anxiously waiting for Jacque. They were excited about riding to school. They liked the way the bright sport's car changed them instantly from nobodies to stars! Nobody they knew had a ride as cool as the one Jacque was driving.

The television news was on, but neither paid attention to it. Suddenly, Chris yelled, "Marcus look!" Marcus immediately recognized the face of his grandfather's friend. "Why's she on tele . . .?"

The reporter continued, " . . . we have been informed by an unnamed source from inside the department that Mrs. Violet Johnson, who has been the main suspect of a major drug, prostitution, and gambling, operation, was shot and killed by city police moments ago. Full details are not available at this time, but we are told that the late Mrs. Violet Johnson was the sole proprietor of a very upscale restaurant in the heart of the city's business district."

"Repeating, Mrs. Violet Johnson has been gunned down and killed inside of one of the city's newer and fashionable hotels. According to unnamed police sources, she had been identified in a multi jurisdictional investigation. We will stay on top of this story. We will update this story and others on our award winning noon report. This is your news channel . . ."

The boys were stunned.

Jacque and Michael had followed Virginia to her place as she had invited them for coffee. Her kitchen television was on but no one paid attention to it. Jacque asked Virginia if he could call the boys to be sure they were ready to go to school. He chuckled to himself as he thought about how disappointed they would be when they found out he would no longer be driving the car.

The sudden ringing of the telephone surprised and frightened the boys. Marcus hesitated to answer the telephone as he recalled that terrible day that they were notified by telephone that his parents were dead. Chris watched anxiously as Marcus answered the telephone.

"Hello," Marcus almost whispered as Chris watched him silently. Marcus began to scream, cry, and speak very rapidly as Chris jumped! Chris found himself cowering in a corner of the kitchen. He did not know what to do!

Jacque blasted through the door with Michael and Virginia close behind. Arms outstretched, Jacque and Marcus ran toward each other as Chris watched. Jacque continued to comfort Marcus as Chris watched. Michael grabbed Chris, joined them praying softly as Virginia rubbed Jacques' back.

It seemed to Jacque that he was carrying the whole world on his shoulders. He stood up, and then flopped backwards on the couch. Virginia sat next to him and began again to stroke his back. Michael volunteered to take the children to school as Jacque glared aimlessly at the wall.

"I am so sorry, Jacque," Virginia began softly crying, "maybe, just maybe, it's, um, maybe it is one of the coincidences, I mean, I don't know what I mean, except, I love you, Jacque . . . and . . ." realizing what she had said, Virginia stood up, walked to, and looked out the window. She looked at the reflection of a very embarrassed and confused woman.

Jacque or the boys may not have heard her, but her confession caught Michael by surprise. Jacque was now crying as he realized that the last time the boys had seen him was with his beloved Violet. What a fool?

Meanwhile, Naomi, who had decided to leave early, was show-ering and singing. She pranced, danced, and sang her way out of the back door. She continued to party as she approached the "dragon wagon" (an untraceable, disposable vehicle). As she turned the corner, the police were arriving.

Racing toward I-95, she stopped at a fast food restaurant drive-thru. An acquaintance that knew about her mother being killed, desperately wanted to be on top of the gossip. She did her best to flag Naomi down, however, she was ignored. Naomi laughed as she waved at the woman, as she was sure the woman had some "words for her" that she really did not want to hear.

Careful to obey all the traffic laws, which were very different for her usually heavy-footed self, she noticed she was 174 miles from New York. There was something, some messages on a Phyllis Hyman CD that made her decide that this was going to be her last trip. She felt a surge of power as she also decided to get out of the trade. She laughed aloud, "Violet can do one of two things. She can like it or lump it. If she likes it or not, she can raise hell or just blast me! But whatever, it is over! Done! Finished!"

Driving the kids to school was a real adventure to Michael. Marcus, Sonia, and Chris only asked him about a million ques-tions. And before he could answer one, others replaced it with another. Arriving at school, they thanked Michael. He promised them that he would always be no further away than the telephone. Watching them walk toward the school, Michael began laughing, however, as quickly as he began laughing, he starting crying.

It seemed like everybody and their mama started crowding into Deloris' office. She had begun writing her report, but the crowd made that impossible. The crowd included her commander, a deputy state's attorney, two F.B.I. agents, an assistant U.S. attor-ney, and a couple of other Feds. After the introductions and flash-ing of badges, they all seemed to agree that she had compromised a long and costly investigation by killing the chief suspect.

Gathering her, "when we entered the hotel, we had no immediate interest in her, nor did we know she was even there. We were there to interview a person who may be a material witness."

Gazing into the faces of the all white male crowd, who were clearly her adversaries, "I am sure that you with all of your collective investigative skills and experience knew that it was plausible. However, in case I was talking too fast, we went to the hotel on a tip, that's T-I-P, that person we wanted to interview as a material witness was staying there."

"Our encounter with Mrs. Johnson was sudden and quite accidental. And certainly, there was no way for us to know that she would try to kill my partner and me. We . . ." One of the feds interrupted, while checking his notes. "So, tell us, exactly why were you looking for this Ms. Dora . . ."

"So, you knew! All of you knew!" she started softly. "You come in here with all of your might to steam roll this poor black country girl and try to figure out a way to make her responsible for your disappointment, things just happen!"

Totally regaining her composure, "And you, My Commander, don't you have something to say? Where's that open fairness, teamwork, having each backs, we preach?"

"We are in here to do what? Why Didn't I Know?" The old battle wary commander began running his fingers through his nearly all white hair, while looking intently at the 'guests', "Right here is one of the best police officers that I have ever had the pleasure of meeting or serving with. If she were a white male, a good ole boy, they would have put me out to pasture a long time ago! I have been around police longer than most of you have been alive." Laughing, "Long enough for me to slip and call her "colored" sometimes."

"I am damned ashamed of myself for letting you jackals talk me out informing this overworked, underpaid, and under appreciated, and honest, cop, leader!" he was now shouting.

"If she were a white man with the same rank, we, and I mean "we"!

Would we have never even considered having this thing going on without his knowledge? No way! I been around a long, long time and know that's true."

Speaking very softly and looking at her with pleading eyes, "even if we felt that there were improprieties which in this case there ain't a chance in hell it would be her, we would have shared."

Deloris stood and gathered her materials. "You gentlemen can let yourselves out as you wish. I am going to write all of this in my report and send it to everyone I think would want to read it."

The commander looked at his watch, "The press will be here before 11 for their noon broadcast. Now, the worse thing that can happen to me is early retirement which will be only a few weeks earlier than my mandatory."

The assistant state's attorney deciding to press on, "now are you saying that you are in no way involved? Everybody knows you people..."

"Sir, you are so far out of line and out on a limb that I do not believe anyone will be able to reel you in." The commander said slowly and sadly. "Do you agree?" (Looking at the U.S. attorney, who nodded, got up and left the room). The others followed. Understanding his career was over, the assistant state's attorney finally departed silently.

As the commander was leaving, he told her to take a few days and when she got back, the odds were that she would be promoted to commander. Smiling, she said, "You ole white boys are full of surprises."

"I heard that a lot of us ole white fellas spend a lot of nights dreaming about women like you." Winking as he walked out the door. He reopened the door and stuck just his head in, "Deloris, that whole group put together couldn't find each other. I never even considered wasting your time with them. Had I thought they could have done anything at all, you would have been the first . . . so, don't let me see your face in this place for about a week."

"You sounding kinda Black!" she laughed. "See you in a week!"

"One whole paid for week, where's my horse, I'm getting outta Dodge!"

Students were entering the school as Nadine was arriving. As she was finishing her cigarette, she saw Sonia, Marcus, and little Chris getting out of a dark   automobile. Checking her makeup, she stepped out of the car in time to speak to Chris. Speaking to him was good for her, however   it was embarrassing to Chris. Nobody else even noticed.

Nothing could have prepared Nadine for the life changing events of the next few hours. The first event was her encounter with Mr. Franks, who stared at her as if she was the prey and he the predator. He did not smile worth a damn. Finally, he "requested" that she go directly to his office. She could have sworn without moving his lips.

Now sitting behind his desk, "Mrs. Walker when you left here, I wouldn't have given two cents for your career. I was sure that by now you would be somewhere in an unemployment line or worse. I had another kind of talk prepared for your departure from my school."

Knowing that he had her like a rabbit caught in a trap, he paused for a full minute. During this time, she was so nervous that she honestly considered telling the short sucker exactly what she thought of him, and snatch his little butt up, total him, and leave.

Picking up a folder, ". . . and leave you will and must. Those hyenas over at headquarters have decided that you are so valuable that you are being promoted to Vice Principal. I don't know what you said or did, and I am sure I do not want to know."

Nadine was totally blown away. She sat there smiling, then grimacing, then smiling again. Glaring   straight in the eyes, "if this is some kind of sick joke, I am going to whip your little ass like you stole something from my mama! Vice Principal? You could do better than that!"

Taking her very seriously, he gently slide her the folder with the transfer information. He walked to the window peering out to the playground. Clasping his hands behind him and without turning to face her, "Please close the door as you leave. Please get all the belongings you can now, and I will see that the rest is sent to your new school. I wish you all the best." As she was getting up, he turned facing her. She could see tears in his eyes.

"Oh, Mrs. Walker, words could never express how glad, how fortunate we have been to have had here with us, me. I know every hair style you've worn, every dress, even your shoes. I don't know the principal there, but he is getting quite a woman. Things will never be the same without you. Now, go, get out of here before I make a fool out of myself."

She tried to go over to hug him, but he wasn't having it. She, too, began to cry as she left his office. Seeing her crying, those in the office were sure she had been fired; especially, Mr. Amos, thinking it was a good thing.

A young man who was sitting in the office was introduced to her as her replacement. Nadine requested permission to introduce him to her next class. The principal made a Napoleonic gesture. She considered slugging him again.

Nadine walked upstairs for what she knew would be the last time. She stood in front of her class for what she knew would be the last time. She looked around the class and focused on the girl. The girl she was now convinced called her a "streetwalker" which now seemed like ancient history.

Clearing her voice, she began, "I am not sure for once in my life what I am going to say. Nothing like this has ever happened before to me. I don't know where to begin, but it will be brief."

Tracey walked into the room.

"We all make mistakes. But first, I must tell you that I was really looking forward to working with you, all of you this year. I have been in this business of teaching for a long, long time. It has been longer than most of you have been alive. Now, I know that some of you do not like me very much and will be happy to hear that I am leaving here to go to the high school as vice principal. Maybe some of us will meet again when we are older and wiser."

Nadine began to laugh, "Children, I should say ladies and gentlemen, I suppose, but if you remember how totally scared you were when your mother brought you here for the fist time. Well, that's how I feel right now."

Feeling the tears about to flow, "Now be good, my stars. Shine brightly and may you get in life all you deserve. I love you all." Before she reached the door, the little girl grabbed her by the leg, "M's Walker, sorry, can you stay?"

Nadine took a deep breath as she headed out the door for the last time.

She did not see Mr. Franks standing next to her car with a smirk on his face, "The only regret that I have is that I didn't get to that thing when you first got here. I know how you got your new position. I have always known that you were nothing but a worthless wh . . ."

Both Nadine and Mr. Franks were surprised at how hard she banged him! He fell back and bounced off a car, down to the ground! Stunned! He rolled over the ground and as he stood up, Nadine tagged him again! Mr. Franks threw a very hard right cross at this attacker but missed badly. Off balanced, he fell again on the ground!

Mr. Amos who witnessed the "fight" from the front door had to compose himself before approaching them. Now, on the scene, a wary Mr. Franks' eyes darted from one to the other. He cleared his throat while dusting himself off.

"Mrs. Walker, um, thanks you for looking out for me. I'm taking the new medications." He offered to shake her hand. She laughed, grabbing him and hugging him. "You bastard!" she whispered in his ear.

Chapter 15
"All This for Free"

Totally despondent Chris walked slowly toward home from school, fighting back the tears. In the last couple of days he had been left by his mother with Jacque, and his "was been" friend Marcus. Sonia was now running track with Marcus. While running with him around that dusty old track she looked very ordinary and when you got close to her she was even smelly. To make matters worse, Ms. Walkers, whom he loved with all his heart and soul was gone to the high school a few blocks away. Even though it was not much further in distance from where he lived it may as well have been on the moon as it would be years before he could be near her.

When he reached the projects he defiantly sat on his own front steps. He dared anyone to say anything to him about it, although there would be nobody. He knew full well that Dora was not there and was unlikely to be there for God knows how long. Even as he was thirsty, he couldn't think of anything that would deal with it. He was lonely and there was nothing he could do about it. It hurt and there was nothing he could do to make it better, except . . .!

Leaving his books behind, he ran to Jacque's home, who was reading his Bible. Jacque was trying to find answers to many questions about Violet, but many more about himself. When Chris asked him for the key to his home, Jacque didn't notice the tears in Chris' eyes. Perhaps he could not see them through the tears in his own eyes.

Keys in hand, Chris ran to his home, picked up, then threw his books back on the porch and "stepped" inside. He went to the 'fridge to get a soda, but the beer looked better. He reached for a glass, but the bottle of vodka looked better. He started to go lay in his bed, but Dora's felt better. He wanted someone to talk to, but drinking from his mother's cognacs made him sing which was so much better.

Marcus and Sonia had at about that time, stopped pass Sonia's for some of her ". . . very special faucet water." Virginia who was in the kitchen cooking laughed to herself, happy that her daughter was building a real teenage friendship. Marcus went home and was surprised that Chris was not there. When asked, it took Jacque a moment or two to recall that he had given Chris keys. He asked Marcus to go see if he could help Chris.

Marcus darted over to Chris's home. He opened his mouth to call out to Chris, but stopped when he saw Chris' books carelessly thrown on the porch. He picked up the books and noticing the door was opened, slowly walked in. Not knowing what he would find, he called out to Chris in a half whisper. He could see the refrigerator door open. He walked into the kitchen and closed it.

Suddenly, he heard Chris in Dora's room, "singing" 'Amazing Grace' off pitch, out of tune, and slurring the words. He walked slowly into the room where Chris was in the middle of Dora's bed belting out, "ooo-ooo-, ooooooooh, a-maz-zing grace!" and looking at Marcus, "who sent this girlfriend stealing . . ."

"Hey Marcus, you wanna have a drink with me? Is Sonia with you?" He stood up in the bed, offering Marcus the bottle. "We knows she will want to take a little drink."

Marcus was totally speechless as Chris began with tears rolling down his face.

"Ever' since mah mama Dora brought me up to this, this, this place," he took another sip, "I ain't had, got nothing but the blues . . . nothing but the blues" He offered Marcus a drink again. "Nothing, I mean nothing in this damned place makes any, um, what was I saying? Yeah! Any sense. People getting killed right in front of yourrr . . . , police coming in your house grabbing and pulling and asking you questions that, and girls acting like they like you, and funny looking women being your mama's boyfriend, teachers acting like they are your girlfriends, a mother that don't care . . . I don't know where she is . . . and I get all this (stretching out his arms) for free!"

Chris lost his balance and fell face first on the bed where he laid motionlessly. Marcus did not know what to do. Finally, he decided to turn Chris over on his back. Chris bounced up like a spring, "and did I ever tell you, M's Walker, aaaaannnd your daddy that I can't stand any of you're . . . " Chris fell into the bed again. But this time he rolled to the floor. Again, he bounced up, "and another thing, I am a virgin and the way you taking my yy, um, Mar-cuss, why you ain't my friend? How come nobody even likes me, evens my mama? You got good sense, tell me what the hell did I do wrong?"

This time he fell backwards on the bed crying. Looking up at the ceiling, "I thinks I need to kill myself and be with Mama Rosa. She knows and loves Chris, nobody in this place knows or loves or cares about Chris, and did I tell you I am a virgin and it is nobody's business, I mean anybody's business? Mar-cuss! Hey Mar-cuss! I want to kill myself, how I do that? I know you know 'cause you are part Zulu, or something!"

Marcus picked up the telephone to call his grandfather as Chris bit the dust again. By the time Jacque arrived, Chris was up again singing, ". . . near the cross . . . near the cross!" Hey there Mr. Jacque. You wanna have a little drink with the most miserable boy in this stinking city? Certainly not, why would you want to drink with a pitiful soul like me?"

Jacque took the bottle and handed it to Marcus, telling him to pour it down the sink. Chris do you want to talk about it?" he asked while slowly leading Chris out to the living room. "Have you eaten anything? Are you all right?"

Chris started to speak, but fell forward on the couch to the floor, narrowly missing the coffee table. Concerned that he was suffering from alcohol poisoning, Jacque called 911! Jacque went with Chris in the ambulance and asked Marcus to lock up. There was quite a crowd surrounding the ambulance, including Virginia and Sonia. Sonia maneuvered to the unconscious Chris and gently kissed him on the cheek. Sonia wept.

Meanwhile, Tracey was surprised to see Johnny's cruiser, and ran up the steps into their home. She was pleasantly surprised to see him sleep as he worked very long hours. As soon as he opened his eyes, he knew he had messed up big time. He told Tracey what happened. She urged him to call Deloris while she made some coffee and cooked a little something.

He called her at the number he had been calling forever it seemed. Tracey could hear him, "Commander? , What? Who? Mobile?" Not trusting his ears, he ran out the door to his cruiser to use the radio. Before Tracey could miss him, he was in the doorway of the kitchen.

"Well, baby, I know I have done it this time. You keep telling me they need men at your school. Well, I may be available soon. I talked to Deloris who was talking kind of strange. She told me to stay here. She'd be right over."

Tracey assured him that everything would be fine. "If nothing else, lover, we can start banking the money, my father sends." She continued distracting him by telling him about Nadine. They discussed the irony of Nadine's promotion and other things wrong with the school system.

"Something sure smells good in here!"

They recognized Deloris' voice as she exploded into the kitchen. In moments, Deloris was eating the food that Tracey had prepared. Laughing, Deloris invited Tracey and Johnny to join her. As the three were eating, talking, and laughing, Deloris suddenly faced Johnny and asked him for his badge and gun!

"But . . . " Johnny began.

"Don't tell me you can't find it. And while you are at it the keys to the cruiser. I think I'll have more of this! Tracey, girl, you sure can cook!"

Tracey could not believe her ears as Johnny went to retrieve the requested. He wanted to say to her that he had been a good cop and deserved much better. Perhaps, after this morning Deloris had lost all respect for him that would really hurt. He returned to the kitchen where Deloris was finishing her meal, "damned what's happening with you two? You in here looking like the two faces of doom."

Tracey had enough, "you come in here with your greedy-assed self, eating up all our food, running your mouth and at the same time, firing my husband. So, how are we supposed to look? Happy? Elated? What?"

Deloris laughed, "so I guess a desert is out of the question?"

Johnny grabbed his wife.

"Good looking out, Number 1", Deloris laughed as she picked up her radio."Now!" she ordered.

Suddenly the air was filled with sirens, sounding like layers of sirens. Deloris grabbed the hands of Johnny and Tracey, leading them outside. They both were stunned at the sight of the impressive van. After absorbing the information on the van, Johnny asked Deloris "what is a 'commander'?"

Instead of answering, she walked quickly toward it with Johnny following. Tracey decided to stay on the porch. A crowd of curious neighbors began to gather along with a few stopped vehicles. She looked at him smiling, "well, if they didn't know before, they know now." Ironically one neighbor, eased up on his porch and asked Tracey what he had done.

Once inside, Deloris handed Johnny's badge and gun to a sergeant. Johnny knew that his career and relationship with her was about over and was preparing a 'good to have known you' speech. She looked at him curiously, asking him if he were all right. She led him to a desk and asked he to sit down.

"In one of those drawers you will find a new badge and gun, you are now my 'exec.' or as I will call you 'number one'. Now these gentlemen will teach everything you need to know. I don't need to know, as you will. You are my right arm, but if you think you cannot handle it, let me know now."

"Also, unless you plan on being in this thing 24/7, select some people assigned to us as your relief persons. The files are in my desk. Now, let me know if you are all right with all this?"

"Well, Number One, you are now in charge. Kick butts, if you must, but I expect everything that needs to be known about this stuff to be known by you. We can't keep these Feds here forever."

She looked at one and asked how long it took for him to learn how to use all of the equipment. He told her that no one was an expert, but it took about a year to get a real handle on the equipment.

She started stepping toward the door, "you boys enjoy your toys. I am going shopping and take a long bath and dress to kill (she laughed). Then, I am going to figure out how we are going to solve all the crime in this city."

She was still talking when she closed the door. One of the Feds told Johnny that the unit could do as much as most large police headquarters with the advantage of being mobile. He added that the commander's unit was equipped with many of the same features with the additional advantage of being able to top 210. Johnny just shook his head.

Having arrived at the hospital and Chris being treated, the nurse recognized him. "Your son must really like the service here. This is his second day in a row. Is this a follow-up from yesterday or . . . ?" She could tell by the expression on Jacque's face that he did not know what she was talking about. "Sir, sometimes my mouth runs faster than my brain and for that please accept my apology. Now, let's start from the beginning."

A relieved Jacque, responded, "sure."

She explained to him that she could not by law discuss his prior visit but was very interested in the circumstances that lead up to his current condition. After listening to Jacque, she informed him that social services would have to be contacted. Jacque wondered what else could happen on this most challenging day.

Chris had long ago been treated, had dinner in the hospital cafeteria with Jacque and was along with Jacque sleep in the waiting
room. A lady with large glasses, huge earrings, and very glossy
lipstick awakened him. "You are such a handsome young man.
What did bad old Jacque do to you? "

Before he could answer, she playfully hit Jacque on his head,
wakening him. She began, "Jacque this best be either damned
good or quick or both. I got a new young man, was teaching him
how to do those things that come natural to a man like you. When
I got this call . . . "

"So, please explain the situation with this handsome young man
(she winked at Chris, while furiously writing on her clipboard)?"

After a brief conversation with Jacque, she asked him if he
lived at the same place and had the same number. She told him
that she would come PASS to visit but was sure his mother would
be home soon. Before sauntering away, she kissed Jacque on his
cheek, telling him she would certainly come pass to investigate.
As she walked away, she quickly turned her head to see if Jacque
was watching. She laughed to herself, Girlfriend you still got it!"

Charles waited patiently in the lobby of the hotel for Dora much
to the delight of the clerk. The guy thought he was scoring major
points with Charles who in reality was not paying much attention
to whatever he was saying. However, sparks began to fly when
Dora entered the lobby from the elevator.

Charles was standing at the end of the counter with his back
to the elevators. The clerk was chirping like a bird to him, even
though, Charles had long ago stopped listening. Dora could tell
by the guy's jesters what he was doing and got instantly angry.
She rushed the counter as if to attack the clerk. Charles quickly
intervened, keeping Dora from completely going off on the guy.
Charles had to force her out to the sidewalk, after the clerk mut-
tered "stinking fish."

As they reached the sidewalk, Dora for a fleeting moment
thought about Chris. She considered telling Charles to drop pass
the projects to check on Chris. She looked at Charles smiling,

wondering if he would be simple enough to take her and Chris back to Georgia where she could give them some money, deposit his butt and go about her business! She began to laugh when she considered her younger sister would love to have Charles with his no love making self.

Smiling, Charles asked her what she was laughing about. She replied, "Men! You really got to love them." She choked on the cigarette she was lighting. "Look, you know where a good restaurant is? I am hungry and really want to talk to you. I would tell you to turn around and go back to the hotel, but in that room I can get no business done. You make me so hot! So hot!"

Charles glanced over to Dora who was looking out the window. He peeped in his mirror at himself and winked. There were plenty of things he could do, had done without Dora. He was a major player in this town as far as making money in the business world. He was very well connected and had made money for himself, most of his clients, the city, and state. Old money was keeping him from being where he wanted to be. So, as risky as dealing with Dora was going to be, it is going to be. In her hands lay the foundation for him to be a superstar. "Yeah, I'd much rather rule in hell than serve in heaven," he thought. After which, he could care less what Dora did. With the power and money he would make he could easily sleep with women that would make Dora look like a man. He chuckled to himself.

While looking out the window, Dora was pondering her next moves. She was certain that if she played her cards right Charles would set her up in something that she couldn't mess up. She felt that as long as she could keep him "interested," he would look out for her. She even considered having another baby, his baby boy that way she would always be in touch. "Not bad for an uneducated bitch, " she laughed to herself.

Both predators looked at their prey at about the same time. Each was certain that they'd found a real live one and would ride its back until each got what they wanted. Charles decided to take her to an exclusive restaurant at a prestigious country club. "Those old fools will have a natural-born baby when they see Dora."

Meanwhile, back in Georgia where Chris lived what seemed like a forever ago, folk were wondering. Alice was sitting in Glo's kitchen wondering aloud if they had done the right thing by letting Dora Lee take Chris away. Glo responded, "Let her? What we did was like a reverse stickup. We forced that woman to take that innocent child up there with her in the midst of God knows what. I hope that God forgives us, but we did that poor child a real disservice."

Alice continued, "We made poor Chris feel like a real unwanted child. I know Mama 'Liz would be rolling in her grave if she knew how we treated poor Chris."

J.B. followed closely by Bill had come into the kitchen, hearing most of the conversation; Bill asked if they had heard from Chris.

"I wouldn't write or call us either if I were Chris. We ain't sh . . ."

J. B. interrupted, "I don't know about anybody else, but I am going to see Chris. I can leave to go up there in a couple of days. If he is all right, I'll shake his hand and hug him. Then, I will hug Dora Lee and come back happy. But if I feel like the boy is being mistreated in any way, in my truck with him, and he'll be back here by Monday."

They looked at each other. Alice asked where Chris was going to live. They all knew that Chris' return to Georgia was a done deal. They also agreed that the four of them should go. Feeling better, Bill asked the ladies if they needed anything from town. He patted J. B. one the back, signaling it was time for them to leave. He began as they left, "surely goodness and mercy shall follow us . . . "

Sitting in the plush offices of the Hollywood film studio, Christee's hope was that she was not dreaming. She had been greeted enthusiastically by the three gentlemen near her agent. She was told that they would begin as soon as (Oh God she forgot his name) arrived. However, she was told that very seldom did a young actress excite them as much as she had. While they talked among themselves, she relived her flight from New York and the hotel accommodations fit for a queen, well, princess!

Suddenly entered the boss. He walked in the door talking, while everyone else listened carefully. His easy manner, style of talking, and the very suit he was wearing reminded her of a Mafia boss. He along with the director, producer, and another guy whose position she did not know all showered her with accolades.

Still as if in a dream, a very expensive pen was placed in her hand. Quickly, with the business concluded, she was handed a check that made her blush. The men laughed politely, and the man in charge pushed a button on the telephone. Soon, a very attractive lady entered with campaign glasses and offered her one first, then the others. She accepted the toast, took a sip, and placed her glass back on the tray.

She was reminded that they would begin in two weeks and was asked what she was going to do with her time. Tearfully, she replied that she was going to get her little brother. The director nodded, "well we will see you in two weeks. Cindy, the young lady who served us is in the outer office, will make all of the arrangements."

On the parking lot with her agent, she decided that she would spend some time with Chris. Her plans almost made her agent pass out. However, before lunch was over, they compromised on her spending the weekend with him. Excited about seeing Chris, she went shopping. She bought him some boy things, as she did not know what sizes he wore. Back in her room, she knew that Chris should be home from school and called. No answer! She worried herself to sleep, after deciding that Chris was coming with her.

As Chris, Jacque, and Marcus entered Dora's home, the telephone rang for the last time. While waiting for Chris to gather more of his belongings, Jacque looked at the caller ID hoping to get a clue as to the whereabouts of Dora. He gasped when he saw the number and hotel name. "Awe no!" he said to himself, thinking it was Dora who called.

Jerry's wife watched him mope around the sunroom while sipping on his drink. She smiled as she observed his eyes surveying the seldom-used basketball and tennis courts, the seldom-touched trees, and the almost too well manicured grass. She giggled at him as she felt that he was behaving like a very young boy.

Not able to hold back her laughter, "Jerry, Jerry, listen, bad boy, the girls and I will go to the beach, an amusement park, or shopping this weekend. Go spend the weekend with your father.

"Try to bring him back here, if only for a few days. The girls really miss and love him. You know we have plenty of room. And while you are there, find your son and see if you can make arrangements to keep him for a while for now. After, we all get to know each other better and get all the legalities together including the DNA; we will be one happy family.

"I know you have always wanted a son, and that boy sure needs a man like you as his father. I am too old and am not going to mess up my girlish figure birthing another child," she laughed. Then seriously, "Most important, you and that boy really need each other."

She walked over to where he was now seated and kissed him passionately before she left the room.

Chapter 16
Single-handedly

Naomi did not have a clue as to how to sort out her feelings. She was not exactly happy her mother was dead, but not too sad either. What she did know was that she was now marked for death. Although, she was never a major player, her mother's being one was always enough to get her snuffed.

"Loose ends will get you killed every time," Violet used to always say. Naomi knew her mother loved to take care of "loose ends" herself. Violet loved it, because the victims never even imagined they were her targets and died with "that look" she loved. Afterwards, she loved to drink, party, and have wild sex with some unsuspecting guy, like Jacque.

"T.c.b.! T.c.b.! Taking care of business!" she shouted aloud. "Well, Ms. Violet, wherever you are. Wherever? I know damned well where you are. I know they expect me to be running and hiding from their punk asses, but I'm gonna kill me the boss man, Mr. Garlic Breath. You being his ho', you might want him wit you."

With tears in her eyes, she wildly swerved her car around in the middle of the street, almost hitting Deloris. As Deloris gained control of the suv, she flipped the switch. The lights and sirens instantly caught Naomi's attention. She looked through the rearview mirror and seeing the monster suv on her butt, sped off. Deloris in hot pursuit had to slam on her brakes to keep from over running the much smaller and slower vehicle, which totally angered Naomi!

The chain of events, which followed, is still not clear. Perhaps, Naomi reached under her seat and grabbed her huge semi automatic pistol. A woman passing slowly in the next lane heading in the opposite direction sees the gun and screamed. This angered Naomi prompting her to shoot the woman in the left temple, which killed her instantly. The uncontrolled car slammed into a car next to Deloris, who was about to get out of her suv.

Naomi slammed on her brakes and jumped out of her car with the huge gun in her right hand, and another in her left. She shot a man.

She aimed the large semi at the window of the suv with the blue and red emergency lights flashing! As Deloris' head cleared the dashboard, Naomi fired four rounds which penetrated the bulletproof windshield which shocked and scared Deloris. Totally crazed, she raised her other hand firing into a barbershop, killing two more. About the same time, two marked patrol cars entered the avenue with sirens screaming.

Naomi spun and fired a couple of times at the one coming from her rear, killing the driver. The car slammed into her car. By this time, Deloris had jumped out of her passengers' door. Bedlam and panic had filled the streets as Naomi calmly reached in her pocket and loaded another clip in the semi, while firing the smaller weapon at anything that moved. Empty! She threw it through the window of a parked car.

By this time, the air was filled with sirens from various emergency vehicles including the strike van. Deloris now had a clear shot at Naomi but would not fire, as there was a woman directly behind her with two small children and a baby in her arms. However, the officers to her left did not take the same precautions, and Deloris watched in horror as the woman carrying the baby slammed backwards on a parked car with enough force to trigger its alarm. By this time, the street was filled with patrol cars; officers and bullets buzzing around like a swarm of rabid bees.

Now standing directly in front of Naomi, Deloris aimed her weapon directly at her, who in turn, pointed her weapon at her and smiled. As Deloris fired, she could see her lips move. They were about five feet away from each other, Deloris thought she heard her, "Our Father . . . "

"Who in the hell is she?" Deloris screamed while surveying the havoc filled streets. She surveyed the total area including the skyline in order to confirm she was acting alone. Satisfied she placed her weapon in her holster as she slowly walked toward the body of the woman. A Para had checked her for vitals and was covering her up. An officer had already taken the weapon, placing it in a plastic bag. The high tech weapon was a research prototype and unavailable to everybody.

Johnny began, "she sure looks different now. Why she is smiling?"

"You know her?"

"You do too! She is, was Violet's daughter, remember the restaurant?"

"Oh my God!"

"Well, Commander, you may have single-handedly wiped out the blood line of one of this city's most dangerous crime families. Congrats!" She walked away from him expressionless and speechless.

One of the commissioner's loyalist, who lived in a nearby county very close to him, called. He told the man about the confusion at the scene, the deaths which included two-three officers and several civilians. He also offered that the department was going to take a big hit for the action of the new Negress commander. He also offered, "just like I say down at the lodge, they don't have the brains or skills to do anything but follow orders. Hell, you sure gonna to be a hero to young and old, everybody."

"Thank you, Bob, Jesus Christ! You know all the time ya' done, it is about time you made Sergeant. Tell Sue to arrange a party for you down at the post!" The commissioner hung up the telephone and paged his secretary.

Within the hour, the commissioner held a news conference! He blasted the new commander for her " . . . disregard for the safety of the citizens of . . . reckless endangerment . . . and the direct cause of several deaths both civilians and sadly her fellow officers . . . and all this in less than a day." Red as a beat, he continued, " . . . and her shift is not even over."

During the question and answer session, one reporter asked about her future. He responded, " If the girl has any dignity she will resign."

Before he could get back to his office, thousands of calls had overwhelmed the department's and city hall's telephone systems. National and international news media were preempting programs.

He was prouder and felt more important than he could ever remember as he recognized the secret number of his lodge commander. They agreed that he had struck a blow for honest folk. The secretary stormed in his office, "...the mayor is demanding that you take his call. And thank you, John, Mr. Idiot Redneck! I am packing my stuff now and beat the rush out of here!" She slammed the door behind her!

He took a deep breath and picked up the direct telephone to the mayor. The mayor shouted, "... get your red neck ass over here as fast as possible, no faster! Throw all your personal shit in a box, paper bag, or throw it in the trash! But be sure to bring your reading glasses with you. We will have a statement for you to read to the press. For the city's sake, we will do our best to allow you to leave town with as much dignity as possible. And, in case I forget, we would really appreciate it if you never set a foot in our city again!"

"What I do?" he complained in the now dead telephone.

Across town at Eric's, two dark limousines eased to the curb. From the first sedan, the four well-dressed occupants, three white men and a woman wearing black expensive suits, quickly jumped out and carefully surveyed the area. Satisfied the area was secured, they swiftly walked to the rear door of the second limousines. The woman opened the door. One passenger got out and looked around. When satisfied, he nodded and the man emerged.

As he began to walk to the door, the woman opened and walked in the door first. The two drivers retreated to the sedans.

For the time of day the place was well crowded. Virginia was scared when she saw the well-dressed armed woman enter! As the others entered, everyone knew it was about to hit the fan as the only white folk who ever came there were salesmen and these people sure were not...

Eric knew who was in charge as the man was wearing a gray suite that appeared to cost thousands and his entourage in mortician black.

Eric began, "Good Afternoon Folks! Welcome to my humble little club."

The man looked Eric in his eyes with a cold stare. The woman reached inside her jacket and pulled out a large cigar tube. She gently placed it in his mouth and threw the tube on the floor. She, then, took out a large gold cigar lighter, while waiting for him to clip off the end. He never took his eyes off of Eric. Eric grabbed an ashtray for him to deposit it.

"My associates and I decided to come here to have a little party with you people," the man began with a benevolent smile. He looked at the woman, "...come here." She walked toward him. When she was close, he nodded at the man closest to her. He knocked her to the floor. "While you are down there, pick the tube off of our friend's floor. She obeyed mechanically.

"Now, go give the attractive lady behind the bar some money, so we can get this party started." She walked over to Virginia, and pealed off five $100 bills. The patrons cheered as they disposed of their drinks and ordered more expensive ones. Still without expression, "get this party started. Drinks and whatever else they need to party we will pay for. If you need more money, let me know. Here's your tip." She handed Virginia three hundred dollars.

At a secluded table, the man and Eric sat talking, very friendly at first. "Well, Mr. Eric, what is this jig joint here worth to you?"

"What do you mean?"

Now agitated, " I always say, you try to be nice to . . ." he stopped. "Let me treat you to a drink that is silk flowing down your throat, like . . . well, just wait." He nodded to one of his gangsters who immediately walked to the door. As he reached the door, Johnny was entering. The arrival of the two sedans did not go unnoticed. Johnny and a female agent entered as the patrons were partying. When told that everything was free, they appeared very happy. However, as he surveyed the bar, ordered a drink, and recognized one of the men as an employee of the late Violet.

He did his best to conceal himself from the man as the other henchman returned with two bottles and a large black cloth bag.

Before arriving at the table, he handed a bottle and the bag to one of the other men. At the table where Eric and his new best friend were seated, he carefully placed a gold cup in front of the man and a dark green bottle in the middle of the table. Eric watched this ceremonial mumbo-jumbo with silent amusement. He got up, walked to the bar and asked Virginia for a glass of water. She whispered that she was " . . . scared to death!" He stroked her hand to comfort her, while the patrons were partying back!

Eric turned to go back to join the man and made eye contact with Johnny. Johnny slowly shook his head "no." Eric turned to Virginia, grabbed her hand, "Everything will be fine."

He returned to the table to join, the now, very disturbed man. "I came here myself to show you respect. I even patronized this, this place of yours that you should beg me to take off of your hands." Eric looked at him blankly.

"Look, with all your valuables in here, what is this jig palace worth to you? Give me a number, if I like it you get it, take your barmaid and her girl, Sonia. Get away from here! Have a good life. Now, if you care what these jigs think about you, take the money, pretend you still own this outhouse, and take orders from my associates and me. Are you one of those proud jigs?"

Eric would not respond. However, he was concerned about this man knowing about Virginia and Sonia.

The man stood, straightened his tie, and as he did, his people rapidly deployed themselves in front of the bar, blocked off Eric's office, and the restrooms. The one with the bottle and bag slowly walked toward him like a choirboy to a priest. The man who had been smiling was now, stone faced. Some of the patrons realized what was going on as the gangsters began opening their jackets exposing their weapons.

Johnny whispered in his miniature two-way as he began to reach for his badge and gun. At the same time the man began, "You, sir, have made me very late for my tee time which is going to cost me. In this bag, well, I know you jigs cannot celebrate anything without a barbeque. So in this bag I got enough plastic to barbeque this jig outhouse. Mr. Eric are we going to . . ."

Johnny was now in the middle of the floor. "Freeze everybody, just don't . . ." The female officer had her gun pointed at the head of the man. Suddenly, as Johnny and the man stared in each other's eyes, they both were distracted by a table tumbling. Behind it was a young man they called "Young blood," who snatched two pistols from of his belt! He fired at the man, placing a bullet just above but between his eyes as the police were storming in the front and back doors. Young blood was the second casualty as one of the gangsters shot him, whom the police in turn killed.

A few momentss later, the smoke filled, death filled room was silent. Eric looked at the bar, didn't sees Virginia and ran toward it, which almost got him shot. Behind the bar, Virginia lay face down, face down but crying silently. Eric cried, then picked up a bottle and gulped down a swallow. Johnny sat in a chair, and slipped his shoes off, "my feet hurt."

In the mayor's outer office, Deloris witnessed many people walk in and out. She did not want to start getting paranoid, but it seemed that everyone looked at her oddly. The secretary took great pains to assure her that everything was fine. As she was asked to enter the mayor's conference room, representative crews from the local media stormed into the room. The mayor looked tired, beat, and only a couple steps ahead of the undertaker.

However, when signaled he was on the camera, he became a dynamo! He began, "...this afternoon, our police commissioner suffered what our doctors are calling a, well I am not familiar with the medical terms, but... a breakdown of major proportions. We pray for his recovery and for his family and many friends. We will keep you informed of his condition.

"Now, we have decided to do something which perhaps has never been done in history. This afternoon we promoted this fine officer to head a federally financed crime strike force. She was selected because of her ability to understand a situation and quickly provide a solution. She manages to do this with the fairness and efficacy that makes her the envy of and at the same time the respect of all who carry badges. Also, we feel that the citizens, everyday people feel better and safer with her on the job.

"This afternoon we told you that she was the highest paid either female or police, um, person in the country. In an unprecedented move by this office and the city council, beginning immediately we are firing you as commander of the new strikes force, and appointing you commissioner. We will not take "no" for an answer."

Michael and Juanita watched the special news bulletin. "Well," Michael began playfully, "you know she always liked me. I may get you locked up! One thing for sure, the streets are really in trouble now."

She responded, "it is going to take much more than her as commissioner to trouble these waters. And as far as her liking you . . ."

Johnny missed the news as he was being taken to city hall with all do dispatch. When he arrived, he was taken to a seldom-used office where Deloris was talking to other high-ranking officers. He entered wondering what was going on. She motioned for him to come sit at her side as the meeting was ending. Some came over to congratulate her, which she accepted graciously as others just left.

She looked up at him, "I don't know whether or not you have heard, but I am the brand new commissioner and you, sir, are my chief exec. You have from now to Monday to go to headquarters, fumigate it! I want Sharon to head the strike force. We are now officially "toothless tigers" as we have both been involved in shootings and you know the deal.

"Whinestart is in charge until I get back Monday after next. Don't ever be afraid to talk to him as we think just about the same way. After the brass gets used to me being in charge, I believe we are going to have a great department."

As the totally exhausted Deloris walked away, Johnny turned his chair to the window. He looked down on the city, then leaned back in his chair and waited for the day to catch up with him.

The bar was now empty and quiet, except for Eric and Virginia. Virginia thought she would never stop crying. Eric began believing Virginia may have been in shock, "You know this is not over. Soon as things calm down a little, they will send somebody else here with an offer. I am so tired of being scared. Scared for myself and scared for you, Virginia. Maybe, just maybe we could start something somewhere else. Just you, me, and your girl."

The strike van was positioned on a high point of the city surveying it. Scanning a small isolated park, one of the younger lieutenants thought he recognized his middle school teacher's car. Laughing, he pointed it out to one of the Feds, "Don't know how it got there, but it sure was not stolen."

The fed pointed at the "hot screen," "looks like quite a party going on in there, better send a unit to check it out."

Virginia finally realized what Eric had said. She liked, respected, even admired Eric, but always managed to keep him and love on different pages. He had always been there for her, but she was looking for. The hell was she waiting for? No way she was ever going to do any better. She loved the way he said, ". . . just you, me, and your girl . . ." but did she love him?

The cruiser slowly approached the small park. The two female officers eased out with their weapons drawn, approaching the car. On the back seat they saw what appeared to be a middle-aged woman and much younger male almost nude and absolutely sexu-

175

ally involved. They ordered the two out and called for instructions. Angrily, the young officer screamed, "hook them both up! Don't do anything until I get there! You understand?"

He recalled, as if it were yesterday, his making a mistake with diction or something. He felt bad, because he really had a crush on the very attractive teacher. However, she turned blood red, telling him that boys like him would never be anything! Almost with tears in his eyes, he recalled her saying, "the only thing you dark ones are good for is . . . nothing! Just get out of here! Go next door until this period is over. Wasting my time!"

On the scene, he looked at her with more anger than he thought he was capable. The responding officers were mothers and wanted a moment alone with this predator. As much as he wanted to let them, he had to maintain the highest level of professionalism. One told him the woman wanted to take full responsibility and let the boy go.

Nadine remembered him and wanted to say something to him, perhaps how proud she...

"Read it to her and transport. Contact his parents and juvenile services. Just do your job, I'm proud of you and will note this in your jackets."

"You know her. But don't you want to say something to her?"

"I thought, really thought I did, but there are no words."

Virginia looked deeply into Eric's eyes, seeing nothing but love for her. "A woman like me would be crazy to turn a man like you down. Scared? You are the bravest man I know. Sonia may never call you 'daddy', but I sure damned want to call you 'husband'. Kiss me."

After a very long passionate kiss, she pushed him. "Man! You should have done that a long time ago. I like that! You something!" Eric locked the door, turned on the closed sign and kissed her all the way to his office

Dora and Charles were still trying to put a good face on their individual plots. Dora smiled at Charles, "Baby, let's go eat and have a few drinks. There is this restaurant downtown that I really want to go back to. You want to go downtown Baby?" Dora began to and could not stop laughing.

Charles waited for her to stop laughing long enough for her to give him the directions. However, when they arrived, it was closed. Still amused with her, she asked him if he wanted to go uptown. They both laughed as she gave him the directions to Eric's. Dora realized immediately that Eric's was closed which surprised her. She thought about dropping past to see Chris and finding out from Virginia the reason the club was closed.

"Where to now?" Charles asked.

"Let's go back to the hotel. Think you can find your way back downtown?" Dora again began laughing. This time Charles joined her.

Chapter 17
Peace Be Still

Now in Jacques' kitchen, they were quietly eating hotdogs, pork & beans with maple syrup, warmed hotdog rolls and grape kool aid. Finally, Chris broke the silence, "I'm sorry I acted like a fool. I was not raised that way. My grandmother would be very disappointed with me. Mr. Jacque, Marcus, I promise I will never be any trouble again." Chris was tempted to cry, thinking about his folks down home, but he did not.

Jacque smiled, "if you didn't get in a little trouble sometimes you would not be a boy. Chris, you are a fine, young boy and young boys make mistakes. So, don't be so hard on yourself. You have gone through quite a bit during these last few weeks since you have been here from Georgia. You will be stronger than most. You may even sometimes know what Marcus is talking about. I am sure I don't always know." They all laughed.

Chris laughed, "Make a soul 'crrrrraaaazzzzzy'!" Marcus laughed.

"You boys clean up in here, while I go in and turn on the game. After you finish, you two future baseball all stars come join me."

Soon, the three were in the living room enjoying the game. Totally exhausted, a sudden deep sleep overtook Chris. He dreamed he was in a beautiful garden with huge flowers, vegetables, and fruit. He walked around the garden and sat in a very soft green chair. He looked up at the very bright sun, but he did not feel any heat. He could smell the fragrances of every flower. He saw a bright light move slowly toward him.

Softly, gently, but with resolve, he heard a choir that sounded like the senior choir at the church at the branch back in Georgia, *"Peace be Still, Peace be still."* Then, he heard his grandmother's lead with the strong voice of years ago, "Oh the wind and the rain obey thy will . . ."

Inside a very bright light, he saw his grandmother.

"Chris, I don't have long. Listen carefully as I will not be able to come to you again. Learn all you can, be honest with yourself and all those you come in contact with. Remember, honor Your Lord and Savior Jesus Christ. You will be the new kind of Colored man I've always talked to you about. "Your grandfather and I and more souls than you can count are cheering for you and will always be there for you. We all love you and always remember to pray. Yes Chris, pray or rejoice especially when things get rough, as they will. Your secrets to success will be your strong will to love, serve, forgive, and forget. Love you, Chris."

He woke up with the calm confidence of one who knows. He looked at the television, and the game was still on. He knew he had not been sleep very long. He realized that he now had a dream to believe in and a future with legions of angels led by his grandmother watching over him.

In the sun-brightened kitchen, Michael sat at his breakfast bar reading the newspaper, waiting for Juanita to cook breakfast. He walked outside to his car, still reading, drinking coffee. As he got closer to his car, he saw little Denny sitting on the curb across the street.

"Hey there, Denny," Michael called out, "beautiful day isn't it?"

Denny looked up at Michael, "yeah beautiful for dem that got coffee."

Laughing, Michael slowly walked toward the boy, "remember me?"

"Yeah, you are the man down at that church."

"It is a little early for you to be out here isn't it?"

"Nope, my mama be turning dem tricks all night, and dem don't like me around. So, I been just out here. Got tired of walking and sat here. I like it around here. It is so quiet here."

"Tell you what, my wife thinks she can cook. We have been married for a long, long time, but I am still not sure about that. Denny, do me a big favor? I want you to taste her cooking and tell me, but it will be our secret." Denny agreed quickly. The two cheerfully went in the house to the kitchen.

Juanita smiling, "was he the reason you went to your car?"

"This is the young gentleman, Denny, I have been telling you about."

"Denny, this is my wife, my lovely and loving wife Juanita."

Denny beamed, "She's finer than the bi . . . lady, down at that church."

Michael hugged Denny as Juanita looked at them quizzically.

"And to answer your question (laughing), he was outside waiting. We are really hungry and would love you a lot more if you fixed us breakfast."

"Well," she began slowly, "you are a very handsome young man. I am sure you are even more handsome under all that trail dust. So, you two are going to have to clean up before you can eat in my kitchen. Take him upstairs and find something for him to put on while you two eat and bring me those clothes for me to wash (or burn, she thought)."

Michael led Denny upstairs to his late son's room. He handed him a towel and showed him the shower in the adjoining bathroom. Denny was apprehensive at first but went into the shower singing. Michael asked him to throw him his clothes, as Juanita would want to wash them. He told the boy he would be right back.

However, when he reached the kitchen with the clothes, Juanita directed him to get the sizes of them on his way to the trash. Soon, he returned to the kitchen. Juanita asked him to stay with the boy and finish breakfast. She told him that she would go buy the little guy a couple of things. "....Just like I used to do when Roy . . ." She ran out of the house.

Talking to the space Juanita had vacated, "Rommie's car will be ready today. We are going to give it to Jacque. He really needs a car and Rommie would get a kick out of him having it."

Now, laughing at him, "we will talk when you get back."

Denny was lying across the bed soundly sleeping. Michael decided to let him sleep, placed a blanket over him and left quietly. He hummed as he called Jacques, "How are you this morning? I am going to come pass this afternoon to take you to get the car. Rommie would love for you to have it. I will call before I come pass to get you. I know you will come up with a thousand objections, but that's the way it is going to be. See you later."

"He hung up on me," Jacque laughed loudly enough for the boys to hear. "He just hung up, before . . . I just don't believe he did that!"

"Who granddaddy?"

Jacque just shook his head, "it's about time for you two to go to school. Here's some money. I didn't have time to fix lunches."

Dora rolled over Charles to the floor. She jumped up laughing and gyrating to the beat of the music! "I'm going to turn you out like a punk in prison. Come on over here and do a line."

Charles opened his eyes and wished he had not. He found himself in the cheapest room imaginable which about scared him to death. Loud thumping music playing made the cheap furnishing shake, rattle, and roll. It had several old televisions none of which looked like they could work.

Surprisingly one did and was showing some hard-core pornography.

The last thing he remembered was going to a place, a bar. Yes, a bar. They had a few drinks out front. They went to a back room to party with some people. He remembered her driving his car. He, also, remembered her feeding, No! Putting the stuff to his nose, forcing him to sniff. He recalled her jumping on him, saying something about " . . .him being her bitch . . ." and some kind of " . . . limes . . . lines?"

"Over here, baby." She gestured while doing a seductive dance. Charles as if in a trance, stumbled over to where she was and fell at her feet. She laughed, "Not yet, baby boy."

Later, in the hospital, the doctor told him how fortunate he was that the fire department got an anonymous call from some lady. As the doctor finished, a detective introduced himself and questioned him. The reality of dealing with the beautiful but potentially deadly Dora began to kick in. The more the detective talked, the dumber Charles felt.

Feeling like she should be celebrating for saving Charles life by calling the paras, Dora cruised the streets in his car, looking for some party people.

As the three arrived at school, it seemed like there was more excitement than usual. The news of the arrest of Mrs. Walker had the whole school buzzing. Many were happy and making jokes about her.

Tracey had spent much of the evening and morning praying for Nadine. Johnny confirmed that things looked " . . . very badly for her." The girls were now with their father.

Meanwhile Denny had awakened and came down to the kitchen with one of Roy's shirts on which was much too big for him. Denny looked around the kitchen, "where is that man?"

"What man are you talking about?" Michael asked smiling as he was warming Denny's breakfast. "The man that handed me this shirt and said I was going to really like it here. I put the shirt over my head and he was gone. Didn't he come down here?"

Michael wept silently without Denny noticing.

It did not take long for Chris to hear all the Mrs. Walker jokes he wanted to hear. He was wise enough to refrain from reacting. Nobody talked about her scratching him. Nobody knew how much he loved her.

It was about 11 when Michael and the very clean Denny arrived at Jacques' home. "Who is this young gentleman? I am sure we never met, I most certainly would remember," Jacque laughed as he opened the door. Michael introduced the two. Jacque offered Denny a glass of milk and an orange, asking him to sit on the porch while he and Michael talked.

After a short while, they came out, collected Denny and drove toward his home. Earlier when Denny and Michael stopped pass, his mother was not home. There was a guy sitting on the steps who terrified Denny. Michael would not leave him there.

As they turned the corner, Denny saw his mother. They made eye-to-eye contact, which angered her. The frightened little boy grabbed and squeezed Michael's arm as he began to cry, "don't let her kick my ass!"

Michael assured him that she would not. Jacque stepped out the back seat and leaned against the car. Michael got out the car, followed closely by the very frightened child. Denny's mother, "I don't know what this little Negro told you, but I never touched him."

"Miss? Mrs.?"

"You going to lock me up for what he says?" Denny was now hiding behind Michael as Jacque laughed.

Michael explained to her that they were not police, which relieved her. She talked about how much trouble he was and that she needed some help with him. She told him the boy was so much trouble that she told him to go find a preacher. Jacque laughed, telling her that he was an obedient child as he did find one of the finest ministers in this city. Michael asked if they could go somewhere to talk. He suggested lunch and offered to pay.

They went to a nearby restaurant and discussed Michael keeping the boy temporarily until she got things straight. He offered counseling from one of the church ministries. She told him that she would think about it. Jacque offered that he had a friend with the child protective services, and Michael added he would speak to his attorneys. While the adults were talking, the very happy Denny ate all of his and much of their food.

In the school cafeteria, most had all but forgotten about Mrs. Walker. Chris needed to talk to someone about her. Marcus listened intently and said very little. Sonia, on the other hand, snickered as she kissed him on the cheek. She laughed, "I'll be damned! You sure are Dora's son!"

She looked at the expression on his face. "Oh Chris, I'm just messing with you. I'm sorry."

When the bell rang, Chris would not move. Marcus and Sonia tried to convince him to go to class, but he would not. The principal asked them to go to class. Reluctantly, Marcus and Sonia obeyed him, but Chris would not move. The principal sat across from him.

"Well, Chris this has not been a great beginning for you. I want you to know that we will do everything we can to keep you safe, provide a great education, and make sure you get on and stay on the honor roll. I have studied your records from Georgia and made a few calls, if things go as well as I suspect, you may be leaving here sooner than your classmates. (He stood and walked around the table to Chris.) Do you have any questions or anything you want to say?"

Chris smiled, "No, Sir."

"Well, hurry up, get to class. Remember you can talk to me any time."

The man, the genius, who promoted Nadine was cleaning out his desk Shala and Natra sat quietly in their father's well-appointed living room. He had decided that they would not go to school. The girls loved their father, really loved their visits with him; however, they were sometimes anxious as he was a very conservative businessman and political figure. Neither could remember ever seeing him without a tie. Also, he had a very deep baritone voice that sometimes sounded like thunder. Their father was not much fun!

"Girls we were not prepared for this, and at this point do not know what we can do to help your mother. My legal people have advised me that she may be away from us for a while. I believe that whatever she did was out of loneliness, and we should do everything we can to support her."

The girls asked him if he thought she was 'sick'. They asked about school, their living arrangements, and if they would be able to see her. In a surprising move, he took off his tie, "I think I will get each of you separate apartments wherever you wish, and . . ."

The girls jumped gleefully, jumped up and down, "Daddy, Daddy, Daddy!" They ran over and hugged their laughing father (which was really usual for him). He hugged both, "I am not ready to, or should I say this town is not ready for you two to be that loose. Got you! You know you already have rooms here. Sorry girls for that little joke!"

Standing in the doorway with a loving smile was his wife. She was happy to see them having fun. He asked her to join him, "We are going to be a family now. There will be some changes, but we will talk   first. I will do my best to be a great father, but I will need your help."

The four began to talk and decided they would do what all women did to get to know each other, go shopping!

As Charles lay in the hospital bed, he again reviewed his recent past with the realization that nothing good could come associating with Dora. He laughed as at the rate he was going he would be dead broke, dead or both.

"Let me see," he preached to himself out loud, "I have been damned near killed at least two times, maybe more. I've been drugged, maybe. I am turning into a junkie. From the way she acts and talks, I may have some incurable STD! And God knows, whom all that money really belongs to. They may be hunting Oh and us! Not to mention, if they find out about this at the office. First, I'll have to pay the hospital bill myself."

Suddenly, he sat up in the bed! "Dora has my car." He moaned.

The detective walked into the room, "look I have checked you out. The best thing for you to do is to leave here, go home, and stay away from the person you were in that flea factory with you. I am not going to waste any time writing reports, and I really never want to see you again. I've got more to do than mess with some Peter Pan . . ." he looked at Charles with disdain.

Totally exhausted and high, Dora pulled into the near empty parking lot of the projects. She grabbed the case and walked toward her home. In her bed, she slept like a baby.

Michael watched Jacque driving the late Rommie's car, "well, when you go out job hunting, you better park this around the corner somewhere." They both laughed.

"Wait a minute," Michael interrupted, walked to his car and returned, "here is today's newspaper. Now, if you cannot find a job you like quickly, give us a call. You know, call the church as soon as you can our secretary is good at finding jobs for folk."

Jacque watched Michael, and the very happy Denny drive away.

Jacque totally enjoyed riding home in the late model luxury car. He played and sang along with the expensive audio system. When he arrived home, he noticed a similar automobile on the lot. He sat there for a while surveying the 'want ads'. As he walked towards his home, he and two men almost collided. They watched Jacque walk to his home not noticing them.

"Yeah, I'm sure," one of the apparent junkies said to the other, "I keeps my eye open and I sees ain't nobody in there. The woman ain't never home, and the boy in school. Ain't nobody there, but we can do it now."

"You sure?"

"Hell yeah, is seven up?" as they eased around the back of Dora's home. They reached the back and decided to climb up to and enter the kitchen window. Jacque thought he heard a noise out back but dismissed it. They had little trouble getting in. Dora believed she heard a noise. Still high, she slid out of the bed. She looked around at her bedroom while hearing voices in her living room. She reached under the mattress and pulled out the .357 one of her men gave her.

She shook her head closed and opened her eyes. She saw the little park that had been her school, where they had carried Miss Scott off. She looked in her hand where she had the .357. The guy in front began to beg her not to shoot him. He said that he and his friend would leave and never come back. "Just please don't shot." The other guy just stood there as if in a trance.

However, in Dora's drug fried mind, she saw him as the deputy from long ago . . . she could feel the heat of the day, the junkie tripped and fell to the floor. Dora saw the naked deputy lying on the ground next to the tree. Dora pointed the gun, the junkie pleaded but Dora heard "Gal, ya better put that thing..." she felt her finger pulling the trigger as she did years ago. The junkie died without understanding what the hell she was talking about. She stood over him, continuing to pull the trigger of the now empty gun. His friend fainted! Jacque, hearing the gunshots, bolted out of the door in time to see Dora aimlessly walking out of her door. He ran to her.

"Dora did you . . .?" he looked into her blank eyes. He could smell the gunpowder and asked her to wait. He cautiously walked to the door, looked in and saw the two men on the floor. He caught up with Dora, "did you, um, about them men in your . . .?"

The spaced out Dora, began slowly, "He needs to stay dead. Don't he know that every time he tries to carry me off I am going to kill him?"

Jacque led heavily perspiring Dora to his home where he called the police. She did not recognize Jacque nor did she know where she was. The first two officers to arrive went to her place; saw one apparently dead man on the floor with a .357 near his body. But what caught their immediate attention was the man walking in circles mumbling to himself. When the others arrived, they decided to cuff and take the incoherent soul in.

Jacque left the very unsettled Dora on his couch as he tried to get the attention of the police. The one who he attracted looked at his watch, as he was dismayed that his shift would be ending soon. He asked Jacque if he had heard or seen anything. After Jacque told him what he knew, the policeman followed Jacque into his home. The policeman immediately called for an ambulance as Dora was perspiring profusely and speaking incoherently. "Put a wet towel or something on her forehead, and the paras will be here very soon. The guy laying next door sure don't need them."

"Why in the hell won't you stay dead?" Dora screamed at the officer. Jacque ran to her as the officer asked him if she was his lady. Jacque shook his head. The paras took Dora away. Jacque volunteered to lock up her place.

What began, as an effort to rescue Chris had become a rescue and semi vacation? What started as two of his kinfolk became eight. They, gassed and packed, were ready to leave very soon in the morning. Glo laughed as she reminded them that they were all heathens, because they wanted to go to Atlantic City. They decided to get Chris, go to Atlantic City and return home without stopping to see Dora again. One thing bothered him or her that was the fact that nobody ever answered the telephone. However, that was not going to stop them from their holy mission to get Chris.

Jerry decided to drive over to spend time with Kingsley. Maybe, he would be able to talk Kingsley into staying with him for a while and talk Dora into letting Chris stay with him.

Christee boarded her flight, feeling good about rescuing Chris. Meanwhile, Jacque did his best to explain to the boys what had happened. He told them that he believed that two men tried to rob Dora. She shot and killed one of them, and the other went in to shock. He believed that Dora also went into shock. He assured Chris that she would be fine.

At the hospital, the nurse asked the female officer if Dora was a suspect. She did not know. "Well, let's assume that she is ill. There are some things we need to do that having handcuffs will make those things more difficult. She does not look too dangerous to me. Does she to you?

She turned to Dora, "are we going to be a good girl?"

"I ain't been a good girl since I was five or six, but I'll be good enough to get this thing over and done with."

During the preliminary examinations, Dora was so cooperative that she, the nurse, and the officer were quite comfortable, even joking and some male bashing. By the time the psychologist got to speak to her, the officer and nurse agreed that she was indeed the victim. However, it was decided that she should stay over night for observation. She was given " . . . a little something to help her sleep."

The television was on; the boys were doing their homework as Jacque wondered what he was going to do with Chris, Marcus, and himself. He was sure that he could get a job, however, after all he had seen and done he wanted more, much more. He needed more. He thought to himself, "you are around here giving advice like you are somebody, somebody really important. Like the man said, if you are so smart, why aren't you rich?"

There was a knock on the door along with the cheery voice of Sonia, "you guys, and I need a little help with this math."

Jacque let her in, saying that the boys would have to help her with the math, as all he could count was Blessings. She blushed when he told her that she was a rose among thorns. The boys laughed as they thought his comment was so old fashioned.

After a while, Jacque rounded them up to take them to get some eats. The kids were prepared for a walk. Chris froze as Jacque stopped next to what was Rommie's car with the keys. Jacque noticed his hesitation and asked him to get in and they would talk about it later. The truce lasted for about fifteen seconds, as all three knew the car belonged to Rommie. After a brief explanation, they headed for some food but not before Jacque asked Sonia to leave a note for her mother.

Denny was enjoying his first home cooked dinner in years. He talked so much that he had to be constantly reminded not to talk with his mouth full. Michael and Juanita were amazed that such a little fellow could put away so much food. As the weight of the food finally slowed him down, he said, "that man told me I was going to like it here." Michael took a deep breath and explained to Juanita what he felt had happened. Her tears watered her broad smile.

Leaning back on his porch, laughing at baseball game was Kingsley.

Chapter 18
The Baltimore Black Sox

As Jerry drove toward his father's home, his prayers were that he could somehow get his father and son to live with him. They had built another wing to the house, so Kingsley could maintain his independence and privacy. Also, there was room, plenty of room for Chris. He could visualize the six of them being a very happy, complete family.

With a naughty smile, Virginia gently lifted Eric's head and kissed him, awakened him. "I could stay with you forever. Eric, why didn't we do this a long time ago?"

Eric hugged and kissed her, "first, be careful what you ask for and maybe it is a good thing we waited. I have wanted to be your's from the time you had the nerve to come in here asking for a job. I think we both had to go through some things before we would be right. I love you, Virginia. Let's really do what we discussed earlier. Let's get the hell out of Dodge."

She snuggled up against him, "Baby I need to call Sonia. I bet she thinks I'm working, but I know you understand. I had no idea it was this late. You are something!"

"Well, since we are going to be a family, let's run pass my place. I can take a shower and change. We can take Sonia out to dinner and run some of this pass her."

They agreed that he would take her home, give her time to bath, change and talk to Sonia. Arriving home, she looked around the projects thinking, "I pray to God that I will be saying 'Goodbye'

191

to you soon and forever." She saw the note Sonia left and began to hum as she went upstairs to take a shower.

As Jerry walked toward his father's home, he heard him fussing and cussing. Thinking there was trouble, he ran to the door."Kingsley, what in the world is going on in there?"

"Son, I so very damned sick and tired of them white folks!"

"What white folks?"

"Them that call the games, acting like they know about base-ball. You see that fool with the headphones? He just finished say-ing that the best team to ever be in this town was the ones who won the 1966 World Series. Now, everybody knows that is not true. You want a drink? I'm going to pour me another. White folks make me so mad."

Jerry always admired his father's passion for baseball and his loyalty to the Negro Leagues for which his father played. He didn't bother answering the drink request as he knew he was going to get one. He started watching the game. The runner was burning a path around third base headed for home. The outfielder threw a strike toward home plate. Just as the runner and catcher were about to collide, Kingsley turned off the television and handed Jerry his drink.

"You know because I have told you a million times that the best team that ever played in this town was the Baltimore Black Sox. In 19 and 29, they could beat any of those white major leaguers, what became this town's bush league team played in St. Louis and came in forth place, I think. Anyway, the Black Sox won the American Negro League Championship that year. They had what would have been a million-dollar infield if it weren't for Jim Crow! At first base was Jud "Boojum" Wilson, Frank Warfield (second base), Oliver "Ghost" Marcell (third base), and Sir Richard Lundy (shortstop). Them boys were so good that they only used the out-field because the rules said they had to have them (both men laughed)."

"During those days, Negro Leagues came and went like the wind. I think two men, um, Rossiter and Spedden owned them.

Anyway, soon after they won the championship they broke up. Then the Baltimore Elite Giants came along in 19 and 33 or 34.

"They had a pitcher, and outfielder named Ernest Burke. Them white folk would not let the Negroes play at the stadium on 33rd Street. They played where that big laundry used to be on Federal Street and Edison Highway. Bugle Field? Yeah, Bugle Field. He told us about all the trouble they had on the road, because of ole Jim Crow. He told us that they once ate at a restaurant those white folks ate in. Well, after the Giants left, them fools broke up the dishes and such so no white folk would ever use them."

During a rare quiet moment, Jerry began, "that's what I came to talk to you about."

"What Bugle Field? Ernest Burke? The Negro League?"

"Kingsley, did you know that your granddaughter began playing baseball this year and is good. I think it would give her additional strength and pride if she knew about the Negro League the way her grandfather tells it. I think that Chris is my son. He . . . (Jerry noticed Kingsley beginning to cry), or rather I will do everything I can to get Dora to relinquish custody. We are going to need you with us to watch your grandchildren and them to watch out over you."

"Okay," Kingsley responded.

"Also," Jerry continued, "my wife wants . . . wait! Did you say 'okay'?"

"Yes! I am damn tired of these projects."

Dressed and ready for dinner, Virginia began to run toward Jacque's as she noticed the yellow tape around Dora's home. She exploded through the screen door where Sonia, Marcus, Chris, and Jacque were watching the game. She asked what had happened and after a while she had the same general understanding that they did.

Virginia asked Jacque to step out on the porch so they could talk. She told him about the situation with Eric. She told him that she hoped Sonia would be excited about leaving, but it did not matter. If Eric would have them, they were his. Jacque hugged her, telling her that he was very happy for them. She collected Sonia and walked slowly toward the parking lot.

"Well, men have patched up the window. In the morning, we will go straighten up. By the way, there was a briefcase beside the bed, I threw it in the closet."

The nurse walked into Dora's room where she was apparently sleep. "Well, girlfriend, it looks like you will be out of here by Monday. I'll see you then."

After the nurse left, Dora mumbled, "I am out of this camp tonight."

In the still of the evening, Dora found a nurse's uniform and slipped out of the hospital. In the parking lot, she asked a guy for a cigarette. When he offered her one, she grabbed his hand asking him what he was doing there. He told her that he had come to visit a sick friend. The next thing he knew, he was walking in the lobby of Dora's hotel.

Soon in the morning, the group from Georgia stopped in Fredericksburg, Virginia to fill up and have Breakfast. They also, called Dora and were not surprised that no one answered.

Denny, who had slept very well, was watching Saturday morning cartoons, a thing he had seldom done in the past.

While Sonia was still sleep, Virginia was in the kitchen drinking coffee and pleased that Sonia had taken the prospect of moving very well. She was a little remorseful about being away from Chris and Marcus. However, leaving the projects made her happy.

Jerry and Kingsley were on their way to breakfast, when they saw Jacque. He explained to them what had happened at Dora's. They decided to get the boys, eat breakfast, come back and clean Dora's place.

At the restaurant, Kingsley's accounts of Negroes in sports fascinated and intrigued the boys. Chris mentioned how hard it was to go to school and play sports with the other stuff that goes on in life. Both men covered their mouths, as they knew it was coming.

Kingsley's voice was so domineering that most in the restaurant looked his way. "Hard?"he began, "how hard can it be. Were you born from, I mean, was your Mama or Papa a former slave? What you have to do before you go to school? Or for that matter, after?"

Jacque and Jerry left the boys with Kingsley while they went to the hardware store.

Kingsley reached in his wallet and pulled out a picture of Paul Robeson. "Do you boys know this man? Bet you never saw his picture in your history books? Can anybody you know tell you about all the things he did and did well? Why is he important to Rutgers University? And tell me why Bugs Bunny got his picture on a stamp and he did not?"

Marcus could not quite remember his name, but Chris did not have a clue. Although Kingsley told the boys he would not tell them anything about Paul Robeson, he was when Jacque and Jerry returned. In fact, there were others in the restaurant listening.

By this time, the Georgia group was passing Washington, D.C.

Dora pushed the man off of the bed. She stared at him and asked him if he had a girl friend or wife or something. The guy laughed, "why you ask?"

"Believe me, you are an all right looking guy, but you ain't shit in bed. So, put your clothes on and let the doorknob hit you where the Good Lord split you!" Dora laughed as he stormed out the bedroom, then slammed the door to the suite.

As Christee's plane was about to land, she rehearsed what she was going to say to Dora. However, she was going to get her brother or die trying.

The sight of the five males walking into Dora's place was hilarious to Virginia. Then she recognized Jerry, "Oh my lord. Where did he come from?"

"Who Mama?" Sonia asked as Virginia was walking out the door.

In a few minutes, Dora's home was full of people: Chris, Marcus, Jacque, Jerry, Kingsley, Virginia, and now Sonia. Jacque was having difficulty cleaning the floor with the crowd paying no attention to him at all. Virginia and Jerry were talking. Kingsley and the boys were talking as Sonia tried to keep up with both conversations.

Dora was about to pour herself a drink when she thought about the money. She was dressed and out the door in moments. She hit the street running, looking for a cab.

The first two taxis at the airport would not take Christee to the projects. The third one, a playa, would have taken her anywhere. By this time, Kingsley and the boys were on the porch talking. Jerry, Virginia, and the very curious Sonia were on the couch. Jacque finished and was sitting in a chair.

The group from Georgia was now in town and asking a policeman for directions. At the same time, Christee had become too through with her cab driver. Dora had finally caught a cab.

Suddenly, Chris' mouth opened and his body began to tremble! Before Marcus or Kingsley could react, he on a dead run headed toward the parking lot where the group from Georgia was walking now running toward him. Tears, cheers, laughter, hugs, and kisses filled the walkway. The folk on the porch and in the home hurried to see what the commotion was all about.

Breathlessly, Chris tried to introduce everybody that was just about organized when Christee bolted out of the airport taxi. The driver followed with her stuff and was finally paid.

Joyous chaos filled Dora's home. As much as possible, the crowd made themselves comfortable with Chris the center of attention.

Suddenly, the place got quiet as Dora was standing in the doorway with a serious expression. As she looked into the many faces, she smiled and with your sweetest southern voice, "I am so glad to see all of you. My goodness, I am embarrassed to be such a mess. I know you think I am just terrible. I am going in my room and freshen up a little. You just make yourselves as comfortable as you can."

Her sisters volunteered to help her. She asked them to try to find some refreshments for everybody. Jacque, Virginia, and

Kingsley volunteered to get some refreshments and hurried to their homes.

Dora resisted the impulse to slam the bedroom door behind her and closed it gently with her eyes darting around the room. She quickly spotted the briefcase in her closet. She opened, quickly inventoried it and took it in the bathroom with her. Most agreed that Dora was taking things very well. The local host brought back all sorts of food and drinks. Somebody turned on the radio. An impromptu celebration began.

After they had been there for quite a while, Dora slowly opened the door. Everybody had to admit she was 'drop dead' gorgeous dressed in the stunning white sundress. She smiled as she looked around the room, making eye contact with most.

She thanked everyone for coming to visit her and with her briefcase in her hand walked out the door. Christee walked to the door behind her. Christee stood on the porch stunned as Dora got into a car and drove away.

POSTSCRIPT:
By Harold P. Jones

Since you reading this it means you done read "NARCISSUS" and maybe the first of this series, "THE WHISPERS of THE STREETS"!

Both books talk about the stuff that happened mostly to, about, around, or near the young boy Chris and his crazy, wild mama, Dora.

Ole Earl done turned out to be some kinda storyteller, liar where I grew up.

Anyways, I done talked to him about the next book and I believe Chris done growed up and stuff done got all whipped up and hitting the fan from all over and it all comes to a head in...

"Chris"

By J. Earl Loving, Jr.

So, what you waiting for?

Go to your favorite book place and order a copy. If they kinda look like they don't know whatcha talking about give 'em that old "po' thing" look! They hate not knowing and will find it for you! Or you can go to Earl himself, try jearloving@aol.com or WhispersIntPub@ aol.com. Write book or the name of one of his books in

199

that dialogue box and I guarantee that he will get back at you!

Before I go 'bout my business, Please believe it is always a pleasure.